DEADLY Gypsy Blue

Bea Carlton

ACCENT BOOKS
A division of Accent Publications
12100 West Sixth Avenue
P.O. Box 15337
Denver, Colorado 80215

Copyright © 1991 Accent Publications
Printed in the United States of America

All rights reserved. No portion of this book may be reproduced in any form without the written permission of the publishers, with the exception of brief excerpts in magazine reviews.

ISBN 0-89636-274-4

Library of Congress Catalog Card Number 90-85184

Dedicated with much love
to
Aunt Bessie Rice
who has been such a blessing and inspiration to me.

Author's Note:

If you should visit Bisbee, Arizona, you will not find a mine called Gypsy Blue—although its appearance inside is authentic to mines in the area—because there are no privately owned mines in the area. All mines have, for many years, been owned by the Phelps Dodge Corporation.

But I was so captivated with the charm and uniqueness of Bisbee's winding streets, the houses clinging to the mountainsides, and the long stone stairways climbing to other colorful streets that I felt compelled to use it for the setting of *Deadly Gypsy Blue*.

Joy O'Clock, who so graciously showed me through her 1906 mansion, the Greenway House—now a luxurious bed and breakfast inn—will recognize her home in the Barfield mansion, Coppercrest, in this book. I hope she won't mind that I moved it from the Warren section of Bisbee to a promontory in the old section of Bisbee.

Other Accent Books by Bea Carlton:

In the House of the Enemy
Moonshell
In the Foxes' Lair
Terror in the Night
The Secret of Windthorn
Touch of the Black Widow
Cry on Desert Winds

If you would like to write to this author, please send your letters to:

Mrs. Bea Carlton
c/o Accent Books
P.O. Box 15337
Denver, CO 80215

1

Elliott Fleet swung his white Porsche onto the pull-out beside the highway above Bisbee, Arizona. Opening the door, he slid off the red leather seat, walked slowly to the edge of the lookout, and stared out over the old mining town. Houses clinging to the bushy, red and grey mountainsides; winding, narrow streets; and Castlerock—a rocky landmark thrusting its rough grey head skyward—lay beneath him.

"What am I doing here?" he asked himself aloud. "I hate this place and everything it represents!" Bitterness soured in his mouth. "If I had any sense I'd get back in my car, shake its very dust from my shoes, and never come back!"

But even as the angry words spilled into the stillness around him, he knew he wouldn't leave...couldn't leave, not yet. The words from his stepfather's terse letter ran like acid rain through his mind: *Elliott, you owe it to me to come.*

"Owe it to him? *Owe it to him?!* The gall of that man!"

Elliott's hands clenched into fists and his throat tightened. "I was never welcome here, *Father*," he spoke contemptuously, as if addressing Cyrus Barfield in person, "so why do you want me here now? What do you want from me?"

Turning back toward the car, he wondered if he would be able to say those words aloud to his stepfather. He doubted it. Even at twenty-eight, and after many years of self-reliance, he still felt a slight quiver of fear when he thought of his stepfather.

"Baron of Gypsy Blue Enterprises," he said bitterly, "with a heart colder than your world-famous Gypsy Blue Turquoise jewelry. If I had been a piece of that gemstone your workmen cut out of your precious Gypsy Blue Mine, I might have been worthy of your attention, dear stepfather!"

A deep ache filled his heart suddenly, and Elliott shook his head in amazement that his stepfather's rejection still hurt him after all these years.

It had been four years since he had seen him, and then only briefly, at his half-brother's, Austin's, funeral. Cyrus Barfield had not even appreciated him coming.

Only Austin, Cyrus's real son, had ever kindled a warm look or kind word in stern, aristocratic Cyrus Barfield, he mused. Austin's death was the one thing Cyrus hadn't been able to control.

Cyrus had always made it plain that he didn't care whether Elliott lived or died, but now he had given him orders to come back to Coppercrest. What was the old man up to?

His stomach knotted as a cold lump formed there—just as it had years ago when his stepfather sent for him to reprimand him for some infraction of Cyrus Barfield's law.

Climbing into his car, he started the motor and swung back onto the highway. Grudgingly, he acknowledged to himself that he *did* owe Cyrus Barfield. The thought rankled but it was a debt he must pay, even if it cut the skin right off his back in tortured shreds!

It was Cyrus's money—Gypsy Blue Enterprises' money—that had put him through school. Cold, unloving, and harsh his stepfather was, but he had promised Elliott's mother, just before her death, that he would finance Elliott's education. And he had.

"I should have known he would someday demand something in return for his money," Elliott muttered bitterly. "And he knew I wouldn't refuse him!"

2

As Elliott drove his sports car into the block-long, narrow lane that led to Coppercrest, he saw a powerful midnight-blue sedan pull out of the garage. When he passed it, he saw a uniformed chauffeur at the wheel. The car waited at the top of the grade until Elliott drove his car into the circle drive.

Elliott glimpsed a small boy and a young woman in the back seat. He did not know the bearded chauffeur, but the man beside him he remembered well: John Howard—the husband of Matilda, the housekeeper—and the gardener at Coppercrest for as long as he could remember.

He parked and lifted his dark eyes to the imposing two-story, red-brick and white-siding Barfield mansion. He drew in his breath sharply. Coppercrest was still as elegant and well-cared for as he remembered—and as cold.

A natural, rough grey rock balustrade enclosed the long veranda. His throat tightened as his gaze stopped on the two large white marble lions that rested on pillars on each side of the wide steps. When Elliott was four, his stepfather had left belt marks on his back because he had caught him climbing on one of them.

Elliott shook his head sharply. He mustn't let old memories make him more morose than he was already. *I won't be here long,* he told himself, *so try to be as objective about this house and its occupants as if they were never a part of your life.*

Elliott got out of his car, crunched up the graveled, flower-lined walk, and started up the steps. As his feet reached the porch, the heavy, carved door opened and a short, round-faced woman appeared. A smile lit up her blue eyes as she ran to him and stood on tiptoe to give him a quick, warm hug.

"Tilda!" Elliott exclaimed. "You still smell like hot apple pie, just like I remembered you." He stepped back and looked at the Coppercrest housekeeper, a grin on his lean face. "And you don't look a day older, but I know it's been at least seven years since I last saw you!"

"It wouldn't have been so long if you had come back to the house after Austin's funeral," Tilda scolded. "I made you an apple pie then, too. I hope it's still your favorite," she said anxiously.

"It sure is!"

Matilda glanced back toward the door and lowered her voice, "I mustn't be keeping you. Mr. Barfield said you were to go right in to the parlor as soon as you arrived." She drew him inside. "But don't you go running off this time before you eat. Do you hear?"

She gave him a gentle push. "Now, go on in to see Mr. Barfield. He's been pacing the floor and growling for hours waitin' for you."

After Tilda had returned to her kitchen, Elliott stood for a moment in the entrance hall. To his left was the ornate main stairway that was the pride of his stepfather. Handcrafted of rich, glowing red oak by skilled craftsmen, he knew the circular staircase had cost Cyrus a small fortune.

Elliott strode down the hall and stopped at intricately carved double doors. As he pushed open one of the doors, the thought came forcibly to his mind that his stepfather only received special guests in the parlor. And Cyrus had never before considered Elliott as special in any way!

A prickle of alarm ran down his back. If Cyrus Barfield was rolling out the red carpet for his stepson, he was up to something!

Elliott's eyes swept the room as he entered. It was all just as he remembered it: the onyx and satinwood mantel and fireplace, decorated with embossed silver and pewter; the settee, loveseat and armchairs upholstered in cream-colored, rose strewn lampas damask; the brass chandelier, with milk-white globes, still hung from the fresco ceiling of hand-painted cherubs on stretched canvas. All of it designed to boast of his stepfather's wealth.

Elliott took another step into the room. His ears caught the tap of a cane, and suddenly Cyrus Barfield was standing in the wide arch of the adjoining music room. Deep shock struck Elliott speechless as he stared at his stepfather. The man who glowered at him was only a shadow of the fierce, erect figure of four years ago!

Thin, stooped, and haggard, he looked eighty-five instead of sixty-five. At Austin's funeral, Cyrus had still been vigorous, erect in bearing and strong in body as well as spirit.

"Well," Cyrus growled, "stop staring at the wreck I've become and come on in and sit down." Without waiting for an answer he took a few short, slow steps into the room and sank into the nearest armchair with a deep sigh.

Elliott felt himself about to stammer as he had often done when he was called before his stepfather as a child. Taking a deep breath, he felt the tension ease, and when he spoke, it was with a calmness and dignity that surprised even himself.

"Good morning, sir. I'm sorry you are not well. I didn't know."

"You would have known if you had bothered to check," Cyrus said caustically.

Savage anger reared its ugly head inside Elliott, and it took a supreme effort to curb the words he felt like spitting out. How like Cyrus to blame someone else for everything! If he *had* called or written, his stepfather would have treated him like a piece of dirt! He had learned long ago to have only as much dealing with this man as was absolutely necessary!

Cyrus finally looked up at him and said irritably, "Sit down, sit down! How can I talk to you standing way over there! Come over here! Sit there," he ordered, pointing to a settee near his own chair.

Elliott again took a deep breath and with unhurried steps moved to the settee and sat down.

"Your letter stated that you needed help from me," Elliott said quietly. He might as well get this over with as quickly as possible and get on his way.

Cyrus leaned his silvered head against the chairback for a moment and closed his eyes. The lids covering his eyes looked like thin parchment, Elliott noticed. A strange feeling flitted through him. Pity? Was he really feeling pity for this man who had never spoken a gentle word to him in his life?

Cyrus opened his eyes, and Elliott's pity instantly vanished. Those tired-looking eyes were as coldly hard and unkind as they had ever been. They moved over Elliott's tall, lithe body, dressed in slightly rumpled but distinctly expensive slacks and turtleneck sweater, down to his casual but equally expensive shoes. The eyes were speculative as they swept up to Elliott's square-jawed, strong face, his thatch of brown hair, and came to rest on the strong, tanned hands that rested easily on his knees.

Elliott felt a pulse beating strongly in his throat but he held himself as relaxed as possible under his stepfather's scrutiny. His own eyes were dark and watchful as he met Cyrus's glacial ones without flickering.

"I need someone to protect Steven," Cyrus said abruptly. He lifted his hand, and it trembled slightly as he pointed at Elliott. "You must help me. I c-can't trust anyone else."

"What do you mean, you need someone to protect Steven? Is someone trying to hurt him?" Elliott asked in astonishment.

"His mother is going to try to take him from me, if we don't stop her," Cyrus said angrily.

"But I thought Lee was in prison."

"She was," Cyrus's voice rose a note, "until four months ago.

She escaped and hasn't been apprehended. I've even got detectives out searching, as well as the police, but she just seems to have vanished."

"Don't you have guards around the place?"

"I did for a few weeks, but then my office was broken into and a good sum of money taken. It had never happened before and I think it was one of the guards we had hired. So I fired them all!"

"You *have* called the police in on this?" Elliott asked.

"Of course! But they haven't found Lee. They offered to send an officer to check periodically, but that's useless!"

"What makes you think Steven's mother is trying to take him?"

Cyrus leaned toward Elliott. A haunted fear showed plainly in his eyes. "A few days after Lee escaped, we got a threatening note. Since then we have received five more, two in the past two days." He hesitated, then went on. "They-they sound—sick."

"Sick? What do they say?"

"I'll let you read them."

As Cyrus struggled to rise, Elliott said quickly, "Tell me where they are and I'll get them."

His stepfather lurched to his feet and leaned on his cane for a moment, breathing hard. "I'm not helpless," he said irritably. "Besides, I keep them locked up. You stay here; I'll get them."

He doesn't trust me, Elliott thought, half amused. *As if I don't know where the safe is.* He smiled, remembering the perverse pleasure he had taken in ferreting out the secrets of this house.

Cyrus brought the notes and Elliott saw that all six were pieces of ruled paper, torn from a spiral notebook. The words were crudely printed with a black ball-point pen. The first four contained the same few words:

"Stevie is *my* son. I'll get him back."

The last two notes that Cyrus handed Elliott both said:

"If I can't have Stevie, you won't have him either."

Elliott handed the notes back to his stepfather. "Surely you don't think Lee intends to harm Steven?"

Cyrus sighed raggedly. "I don't know *what* to think, but it sounds like that's what she's threatening."

"Has Steven's mother been seen around here?"

"She hasn't been seen anywhere! That's what's so frustrating!" Cyrus almost shrieked. "At first I thought she would be found momentarily, but she must have friends who are hiding her."

"Are you sure the notes are from Lee?"

"Who else could they be from?" Cyrus said sharply. "The first note came a few days after she escaped."

"What measures are you using at present to protect Steven?"

"I don't let him leave the house without at least two adults to watch over him. When he has to go to town—like today he has a dental appointment—I send John, the gardener, Allyssa Star, his nanny, and, of course, Marvin, the chauffeur."

"Where do I come in?"

"I want you to guard Steven. I want you with him every moment possible, day and night, until that woman is found and put back in prison!"

"I'm not a bodyguard!" Elliott exclaimed.

"You've been all over the world chasing down stories for your newspaper. I'm sure you have been in some very dangerous situations," Cyrus said adamantly. "Surely you can protect a small boy from a mere woman."

Elliott stood to his feet, his jaw set grimly, defiantly. "No, thank you! You can hire a reputable bodyguard who can do a hundred times better job than I can. Get references! You have money to buy the best!"

"You are refusing to help me when I need you?" Cyrus asked in an icy voice.

"Yes, I am. I'm not cut out to be a nursemaid for a child! It's a mystery to me why you want me anyway when there are professionals who do this for a living!"

Cyrus struggled to his feet and stood as tall as he could.

Elliott was amazed to find that his own six feet, two inches towered over his stepfather. Had the man shrunk that much or had he never been as tall as he remembered?

"You owe it to me!" Cyrus thundered. "I paid for your food and clothes—and for a good education for you. That's how you can afford that fancy sports car and dress like a rich playboy! I gave you your chance! You owe it to me to give me a few weeks of your time!"

Elliott stared at his stepfather, his eyes matching Cyrus's for cold hostility. "And you begrudged every bite I took of your bread and every night I spent in your house! If you hadn't promised my mother to take care of me until I was grown and to educate me, you would have thrown me into an orphanage when I was 14!"

"Well..." Cyrus's thin lips pressed into a wintry smile. "That's the first spunk I've ever seen out of you! And it tells me that I've made a good choice asking you to guard Steven for a few weeks."

Elliott glared at his stepfather, but Cyrus's thin, infuriating smile remained in place. At last Elliott spoke sharply, "Why do you think you can trust *me*? Surely you know I feel no love for you—or for Austin's son."

For a long moment Cyrus locked eyes with Elliott, then he said softly, "You have no love for me or mine, but as your mother's son, you have something better—loyalty!"

"Where did you ever get the idea that I feel any loyalty to you—or your grandson?"

"Your mother was loyal to a fault, and I know you to be your mother's son. You are very aware of the debt you owe me—a debt you know you will repay!"

Elliott felt as if the breath was being pressed from his lungs by the bony knee of this man. How well the old man knew him! The thought made him furiously and frustratingly angry.

"How do you know I can do what you ask? I've never guarded anyone in my life. And I don't even know how to act around a kid!"

Cyrus's words were filled with confidence, as if he knew Elliott would comply with his wishes. "I've followed your career—to your astonishment, I see—and I am aware of your resourcefulness and dependability. When you set out to get a story, you get one. No obstacle, danger, or person deters you. You are the one I need to protect Steven."

Elliott glared rebelliously at his stepfather, and suddenly the old gentleman's voice became almost pleading—to Elliott's discomfiture, because Cyrus's words were affecting him in spite of his determined effort to resist them.

"Elliott," Cyrus said, using his stepson's name for the first time, "I don't know if I can trust anyone in this house anymore. They may all be against me. And I fear for my grandson. He is all I have left. You will help me? I will pay anything you ask."

Elliott stood silent for a moment, feeling as if this man held an invisible but very real knife to his jugular. His voice roughened by anger, he said harshly, "I guess I have no choice, do I? But I warn you, I have only four weeks leave from my newspaper." His eyes glinted as he added testily, "This is supposed to be my vacation after a dangerous and difficult assignment."

Cyrus snorted and said brusquely, "Get your luggage and have Tilda show you to the room next to Steven's. As of now, you are in complete charge of my grandson."

3

Elliott refused Tilda's offer to put away his clothes. He wanted to be alone. Soon enough, his privacy would be gone, with a small child underfoot most of the time, he thought distastefully.

The few clothes he had brought looked lost in the enormous closet. Before he put away his shirts and socks, he gently unwrapped three photos in silver frames, joined together with little silver hinges. Setting them almost reverently on the small table beside his bed, he sat down and studied them nostalgically.

One photograph was a slightly faded likeness of his father and mother on their wedding day. The middle one was his own baby picture, and the third was a photo of himself and his mother on his fourteenth birthday, just a few weeks before she died.

A mist rose in his eyes as he gazed at the last picture. In spite of her thin, fragile body, his mother was beautiful. And how she had loved him! That was the only thing that had kept him from running away from Coppercrest. For his mother, he had endured the harsh treatment dealt to him by his stepfather and the torment his half-brother had heaped upon him.

He had never told her of his humiliations and hurts. Even as a small child, he had known his mother was delicate and ill, and he had always felt he had to protect her from worries.

He recalled vividly his last few minutes with her. She had sent Tilda to call him to her bedside. She was very weak, and her voice had been so faint as he knelt beside her that he still had to lean over close to her pale lips to hear her words.

He could remember them distinctly, "Elliott, be a good boy. Cyrus has promised to see that you get a good education. Take advantage of it because there is no place in this world for an uneducated man. Work hard and become the best reporter that ever went after a story!

"Elliott, I have prayed for you all these years. Don't let bitterness or meanness get into your soul."

Elliott had often pondered those last words. Had his mother known more about his trials than he had realized?

Then his mother had asked him to lean over so she could kiss him. Agony tight in his throat because he knew how close he was to losing her, she had patted his face with a soft, frail hand.

Tears stood in her eyes, too, but she whispered again urgently, "Take the little package under my pillow. They are my special photographs. They are now yours and yours only. Perhaps it would be best if no one else knew about them. Hide the package under your shirt."

He drew it out and slipped it inside his shirt and leaned over her to hear the other words she was laboring to speak. Suddenly her face seemed to lose what little color it had and she struggled to speak, "I have secured your—your...."

Anguish filled her dark eyes—so like his own—as she tried to finish the sentence. Then, suddenly, as if a light was extinguished, the loving glow disappeared from her eyes, they glazed, and then went blank.

Elliott recalled that, terror-stricken, he had called her frantically, but she had lain limp and silent. Blinded by tears, he had sprung away from the bed and run to the door screaming for help. The room was quickly swarming with people, but no one was able to do anything. His mother was dead.

No one had paid any attention to him, and he had stayed until they carried her away in an ambulance. Austin had tried to hold his mother when they took her away, and Cyrus had gently pried away Austin's clutching hands and had held his son in his arms next to his chest while he wept. No one had comforted Elliott.

Tilda had finally noticed him, as in numb but utter desolation and devastation he followed the gurney that was wheeling his mother away. The motherly housekeeper had put her arm around him and hugged him to her side for a moment before she fled to the refuge of her kitchen. He remembered feeling her tears fall on his forehead. Everyone had loved his gentle, beautiful mother, even hardhearted Cyrus.

Cyrus had never offered any sympathy to his fourteen-year-old stepson. He had ignored his presence until the funeral was over. Then that afternoon, Elliott had been summoned to Cyrus's study where his stepfather had brusquely informed him that he would be leaving the next day for a boarding school.

A mist rose in his eyes and a lump in his throat as Elliott remembered the bitter, heartbroken tears he had cried that night. Not that he had any desire to stay at Coppercrest, but because he was being tossed away like a mangy, unwanted puppy.

A few times he had been allowed to return for holidays but the loneliness was worse at home than at school, so very soon he began to beg off and his stepfather did not urge him to come.

A sudden tap at his door caused Elliott to start. "Dinner will be ready in thirty minutes," Tilda's voice called softly. "Mr. Barfield still doesn't like tardiness at meals."

Elliott crossed to the door and opened it. "And I suppose he still insists on everyone dressing up like we are going to a concert?"

"I'm afraid so," Tilda chuckled. "And I still remember how you hated to dress up just to eat!"

Suddenly she looked past him and exclaimed, "Your mother's photographs! I wondered what became of them. You took them away with you."

Was it an accusation? "Mother gave them to me just before

she died," Elliott said.

"Your stepfather had me look everywhere for those photographs," Tilda said. "He even made me search your suitcase for them—before you left for school after your mother's funeral—and also your room after you were gone." She laughed softly. "And you had them all the time."

A slight chill ran down Elliott's backbone. "What did Cyrus want with the photographs? They are of Mother and my father, and of me and Mother. Why should he want them?"

"I have no idea," Tilda said quickly.

Elliott's eyes narrowed. Did Tilda know more than she was telling?

Tilda turned away. "I'd better get back to my dinner."

As he closed the door, Elliott felt something like panic come over him. Would his stepfather demand the photographs—the only thing Elliott had left of his mother's?

He walked over and picked up the pictures and turned them over in his hands. They were small, about five by seven inches, and very ordinary in every way. What possible use could Cyrus have for them?

His mother had always kept them in a drawer in the little table next to her bed. And she had shown them to him many times.

"I want you to remember what your father looked like," she had said. The third frame had held a picture of her deceased parents until she had had a photographer take a picture of Elliott and his mother on his fourteenth birthday.

Although she was weak from the illness that claimed her a few weeks later, she had taken him out to an expensive restaurant for his birthday. What a delightful time they had shared! He seldom had his mother to himself and he was elated.

The photographer came to the restaurant to take the photo of them, obviously by appointment. He recalled the photographer suggesting rather forcefully that she get a large photo, or at least others. She had calmly refused but promised to pay whatever he asked for the one photograph. "I want it for a very special place," she had said.

He grinned to himself as he remembered his joy at having a place in the honored silver frame with his mother and father. And he also recalled feeling jubilant that Austin, his mother's younger son, was not included.

His mother loved Austin, he had known, but Elliott was her firstborn and special to his mother, he had reasoned. It had been so important to him, then, to be special to someone—and especially to his mother.

Suddenly he heard voices in Steven's room next door. He set the photographs back on the table, crossed to the door, and opened it a crack. He might as well get a look at his nephew and his nurse.

Clearly he heard a young woman's voice say crisply, "Now, I'm going downstairs for dinner. Remember, you mustn't leave this room. Marvin will be right up with your tray. He will stay until I get back."

A peevish voice said crossly, "I don't need a babysitter all the time. I'm five-years-old."

"Those are your grandfather's orders, and they are for your own good," the woman's voice said sternly. "Now, do as I say or there will be no bedtime story for you tonight!"

"Yes, ma'am," the small voice agreed reluctantly.

Elliott heard the hall door close with a snap. He opened the connecting door wider, knocked lightly, and asked, "May I come in?"

The small boy standing in the middle of the room whirled around and stood staring at him with dark brown eyes, so like Elliott's own.

"You are my daddy's brother," the child said slowly. "You look like his picture."

"I suppose we do resemble each other," Elliott said, "but I'm afraid I was never handsome like your father."

"Allyssa—that's my nanny—said you were going to be staying in the next room to me—to protect me if my mother tries to kidnap me," he stated gravely as he looked Elliott over speculatively. "You're big and tall so I don't think she could get me away from you."

Elliott saw that Steven had Lee's pale brown hair, as silky as a girl's. And he had her long-legged frame. However, where Steven's mother was a little plump, her son was slim. Lee had been soft-looking, with a pretty, rather pouty face and large golden hazel eyes—not dark brown ones like her son's. But Steven had the same dark brows and lashes as his mother that contrasted with their pale hair.

A quick tap came on the door and Steven ran to open it. A bearded young man entered with a tray.

"You must be Marvin, the chauffeur," Elliott said. "I'm Elliott Fleet, Steven's uncle."

"It's good to meet you, sir," Marvin said formally. A quick smile lighted his bearded face and one eyebrow rose in a quick flick. "We saw you arrive."

"Yeah," Steven spoke excitedly, "that's a grand car you were driving. Would you give me a ride?"

"Sure," Elliott agreed. "And now I guess I had better get dressed for dinner."

"Yep," Steven said soberly. "Grandfather gets mad if anyone is late for dinner. I'd rather eat up here with Marvin," he declared decisively.

"I expect it would be a lot more fun," Elliott said more to himself than Steven. He looked up to see Marvin staring at him with a penetrating, guarded expression on his face.

The chauffeur's dark blue eyes quickly dropped, and he moved away to begin setting dishes on a small table near the window.

Elliott went back into his room and began to dress for dinner. His reporter's senses were tingling. Had he met Marvin before? Not that he could recall—and yet there was something disturbingly familiar about him. If only he could think what it was!

4

As Elliott entered the dining room a few minutes later, all heads turned his way. His eyes swiftly scanned the room, noting the same polished red-oak dining table, china cupboard, and buffet that were here when he was a boy. Surely the copperish-green velvet drapes and matching coverings for the carved, high-backed red-oak chairs were not the same, but the color was. And the antique silver chandelier, with its glowing, soft-white electric candles still hung over the table.

Cyrus was seated in a cushioned rocker near the fireplace, and a very attractive, blonde young woman was leaning over him, replenishing a glass in his thin hand.

It was a slight shock to Elliott to see Gentry Howard standing on the other side of Cyrus, immaculately and expensively dressed, obviously at ease in the formal dining room. He had forgotten that Gentry—son of the housekeeper and gardener, whom Cyrus had also sent to college—was the General Manager of Gypsy Blue Enterprises.

Before anyone else moved or spoke, Jessica, Cyrus's sister and the fourth person in the room, moved quickly to him and gave him a warm embrace. "It is so good to see you again, Elliott."

A genuine smile filled Elliott's eyes. "Aunt Jess! I supposed you were were still gallivanting about the world, spying on hummingbirds!"

Jessica laughed the low, almost mannish laugh that had thrilled Elliott as a boy. Her hair was drawn back in a rather untidy ball at the nape of her neck—just as it used to be, but she did look older. Silver streaked her auburn hair and her amply-padded, tall figure—carelessly groomed, as usual—was a little stooped. But her warm, grey eyes were still as bright and alert as the hummingbirds she tracked and studied so assiduously.

Elliott knew Cyrus and Jessica's father had left his naturalist daughter most of his money, making her independent and able to pursue her passion—hummingbirds. Cyrus had inherited the Barfield business which included the Gypsy Blue Mine and a jewelry store in Bisbee, plus four trading posts on Indian reservations in Arizona and New Mexico. The Barfield mansion was owned jointly by Cyrus and Jessica.

Gentry came toward them and extended his hand. "It's been a long time, Elliott. Welcome back to the family manor."

Was there sarcasm in the words, Elliott wondered. Gentry's hazel-green eyes held no welcoming warmth. Did he feel Elliott was a threat to his position in the business? Well, he might as well ease his anxieties if that were true.

"Yes, it has been a while, Gentry," Elliott said as he shook hands, "but I don't expect to stay long. I'm still a roving reporter for a very demanding newspaper."

"That sounds exciting," a lilting female voice said.

Elliott looked beyond Gentry to see the blonde young woman smiling at him.

Gentry turned to put a possessive hand on the woman's arm and draw her forward, "Elliott, this is Allyssa Star, Steven's nanny."

"I'm delighted to meet you," Elliott said, and meant it.

Allyssa was stunningly lovely, in a wine-colored lacy dress, and matching sandals. Being a nanny must pay well, Elliott thought, as he took in her diamond earrings, matching necklace, and dainty, diamond studded watch.

"Well, we can eat now," Cyrus's plaintive voice spoke from across the room. "I thought we were going to have to send Tilda after Elliott like we used to."

Elliott felt irritation stab at him, but he forced it away. "I'm not late," he denied.

Cyrus made a disparaging noise in his throat and said dryly, "Of course not! You made it with one minute to spare!"

Ignoring the sarcasm, Elliott went over to his stepfather, "Could I offer you my arm, sir?"

Cyrus glared into Elliott's calm, unperturbed eyes for a few seconds and then said ungraciously, "If you like. This dratted cane is a nuisance!"

Elliott led Cyrus to the head of the table, seated him, then drew out a chair for Jessica before seating himself next to her. Gentry helped Allyssa into her chair with the same possessiveness Elliott had noted before. He was amazed that the idea was not pleasing to him.

Cyrus said little during the meal, seeming preoccupied and morose. He only picked at his food and didn't even seem to notice when Tilda accidentally spilled some tea on the lace tablecloth. Elliott wondered if he was in pain.

Allyssa was a sparkling conversationalist, witty and vitally alive. Gentry applied himself to his meal but spoke with ease when he chose to speak. Jessica was her usual somewhat abstracted self, inserting comments here and there, many times completely irrelevant to the subject being discussed.

About halfway through the delicious meal—Coppercrest could never be faulted for its food—Allyssa spoke across the table to Elliott. "I imagine you have had some fascinating experiences in your news jaunts about the world. I would love to hear about some of them."

Elliott was pleased but said deprecatingly, "A lot of it is just routine, of course, but every once in a while I have an assignment that gets a little hairy."

"Mr. Barfield's assignment is a little out of your class, isn't it," Gentry interposed, "being a bodyguard for a five year old—to protect him from a woman, no less?"

Gentry's tone was bantering, but when Elliott glanced at

him, he was surprised to see contempt glint in Gentry's eyes.

"You don't approve of Steven having a bodyguard, I take it?" Elliott asked candidly.

Gentry glanced over at his employer and then said smoothly, "Certainly I'm for him having a bodyguard until his mother is found and back in prison, but a professional would seem a more logical choice than a news reporter."

Elliott saw a frown appear on Cyrus's face, but to his amazement, Cyrus's answer was mild, "I explained why I got Elliott to come, Gentry. I needed someone I could trust. And I don't trust someone I don't know."

"And how do you know you can trust Elliott?" Gentry said pointedly. "You haven't seen him ten times since he was fourteen."

"But I made it my business to know what kind of man he became," Cyrus said patiently.

"It's your business, Mr. Barfield," Gentry said, "but I still question his competence as a bodyguard."

Elliott felt his ire rise. His deepest desire when he got here had been to get his business over as quickly as possible and leave, but he didn't want Gentry—who should have no part in family affairs—deciding whether he could do a good job as Steven's bodyguard.

"Now wait a minute, Gentry," Elliott heard himself saying, "I didn't ask for this job but I took it and I plan to see it through!"

A dark frown appeared on Gentry's smooth, clean-shaven face. He opened his mouth to speak, but Cyrus silenced him with an imperious hand.

Cyrus's voice was sharp. "Gentry, I appointed Elliott as bodyguard to Steven and he stays! There will be no further discussion on the matter!"

A wave of red swept over Gentry's face. For a long moment his green eyes smoldered as they stared at his employer. Then he dropped them, picked up a glass of water, and drank slowly. Absolute silence reigned and the room seemed charged with seething undercurrents.

Then Jessica spoke to Elliott, "Well, I'm glad you are staying. We have seen far too little of you for too long a time."

Ignoring Jessica, Cyrus said to Elliott, "I have had the locks changed on Steven's and your rooms. I want you to lock them—and also the windows each night. And leave the door open between your rooms so you will know if anything is going on in his room. I hope you are a light sleeper."

When Elliott said that he was, Cyrus spoke to the others, "Elliott is to be completely in charge of Steven. Whatever measures he wishes to take to ensure his safety are up to him. I'll make this clear to the servants, too."

Cyrus turned to Allyssa. "Please do not take Steven anywhere unless Elliott accompanies you. And that goes for everyone else, as well."

"I appreciate that, sir," Elliott said. "It will make my job easier."

Gentry said nothing for a long moment as the heightened color receded from his face. Then he looked up and spoke carefully, "You're the boss, Mr. Barfield." He never looked at Elliott directly the remainder of the meal.

The air of tenseness did not leave the room even during dessert, although everyone—except Cyrus, who said nothing more until the meal was over—talked and smiled and tried to act naturally.

When they left the table, Jessica came close to Elliott and spoke softly, "Please come to my suite in half an hour. I want to talk to you. It's important. And..." she looked around to see if anyone was listening and then whispered, "and bring your mother's photographs."

5

As Elliott left the dining room, Allyssa fell into step with him. "We might as well walk up together. I have to read Steven his bedtime story and then put him to bed. Are you going to join us?"

When he hesitated, she smiled—he noticed she had a delightful, deep dimple in her left cheek when she smiled—"Please, do come. Perhaps you could relate an amusing story for Steven from your travels. I know he would love it—and so would I."

Elliott agreed, and to his surprise, the next half hour passed too quickly. When Allyssa announced that Elliott was going to tell him a story—if he hurried into his pajamas—Steven let out a squeal of joy. Elliott told a story that his mother had told to him many times when he was small.

When it was told, the child begged for more and he told another. Then Allyssa firmly told Steven that was all for the night.

"I really must go anyway," Elliott said reluctantly. "I promised Aunt Jess to go down and talk with her for awhile tonight."

"There's a large television down in the family room if you want to watch TV later," Allyssa said. "Also a VCR and a lot of good videos. Gentry is a movie and camcorder buff. You are welcome to come down and join us when your little chat is over."

"Cyrus requested that Steven not be left alone," Elliott said. "So I had better not leave him."

"Oh, we don't ever leave him alone since his mother escaped," Allyssa assured him. "Either I or the chauffeur stay with him, even at night. But Marvin never seems to mind staying with Steven, so don't feel you have to be completely tied to him."

"Then I will probably take you up on some television a little later," Elliott said. *This visit to Coppercrest may be quite enjoyable, after all,* he thought, as he walked down the hall and then descended the rear stairs.

Jessica's suite was at the back of the house, with an entrance of her own. He was almost there when he realized he had forgotten to bring his mother's photographs. He turned to retrace his steps, wondering why Jessica was interested in his mother's pictures. And how did she know about them? Of course the answer to that was that Tilda had told her. But why would Tilda think anyone would be interested in them?

Elliott started to turn the knob on the door of his room when he heard a sound. Someone was in his room!

He turned the knob gently and eased the door open. Allyssa stood by his bed with her back to the door. As he watched, silent and motionless, she turned and started toward Steven's room. In her hands she carried his mother's photographs!

Astonished as well as puzzled, Elliott took a step into the room and spoke quietly, "May I help you?"

Allyssa jumped as if she had been struck by a rattlesnake. "Oh—oh, you–you startled me!" she said when she saw him.

She seemed to regain her composure. "I–I hadn't ever looked into this room. I hope you don't mind me looking around." She smiled then, "Please forgive me for my curiosity."

When he said nothing, she turned to go. "I had better get back to Steven."

"My mother's photographs..." Elliott said.

"Your mother's photographs? Oh, you mean these?" If her surprise was not genuine, the girl was a superb actress. "I wasn't aware they were yours. The whole house is full of old photographs, and I thought these just went with your room. I was going to show them to Steven and see if he knew who the people in it were. Naturally I would have returned them."

When Elliott continued to stand looking at her, not knowing whether she was telling the truth or not, Allyssa suddenly turned around and dumped the photographs on the foot of his bed. "I see you don't believe me," she snapped, "but it's the truth whether you believe me or not! And I'm sorry I invaded the privacy of one of the lordly Barfields!"

Tossing her long blonde hair, Allyssa walked quickly to the open door between the rooms. Suddenly Elliott chuckled and Allyssa turned and looked at him, fire in her blue-grey eyes.

"I'm not a Barfield," Elliott said. "And I'm sorry if I appeared to be angry. But you see, I just didn't know what to think when I saw you walking off with my most prized possession."

Allyssa walked back to the bed and picked up the photographs and studied them. Then she said softly, "The woman must be your mother." When Elliott nodded, she went on, "She is very beautiful. And you look like the man so he must be your father."

Elliott came to stand beside her. "I never knew him," he said, "but mother told me so much about him that I feel like I did. He was a pilot in the Korean War. They were only married two years when he was shot down over there. I wasn't even born when he died."

"Then your mother married Cyrus Barfield," Allyssa prompted.

"Yes, Mother was not well, and she was worried that she might die and leave me with no one to care for me. I was only a month old when she and Cyrus married."

"How much older are you than Austin?" Allyssa asked.

"Fourteen months," Elliott said.

"Maybe I'm talking out of school," Allyssa said softly, "but Gentry said Mr. Barfield never seemed to love you like he did his own son. How could he help it when he was the only father you ever knew?"

"You would have to ask Cyrus that," Elliott said, "but he never loved me and still doesn't. I'm just something he happens to need right now." His voice had gone bleak.

"I really must go now," he said abruptly. "Aunt Jess is expecting me."

"Would you mind if I showed these photographs to Steven?" Allyssa asked eagerly. "I'm sure he would be thrilled to see a picture of his grandmother."

"I'm sorry," Elliott said, "but that's what I came back upstairs for. Jessica wants to see these old photographs. She knew my mother well."

"Of course," Allyssa said quickly. "We can show them to Steven another time."

As he went slowly back down the hall, Elliott pondered. Was Allyssa telling the truth when she said she just wanted to look into his room and innocently took photos she thought were only part of the decor of the room? Surely she had seen the room many times before and knew the photographs were a new addition. It didn't sound too plausible.

But if Allyssa was lying, and she had purposefully taken the photographs, what did she want with them? Strangely, the old photos were of interest to several people.

6

Jessica welcomed him with a quick hug and seated him in a platform rocker near her own chair in front of a cozy, red-brick fireplace. She put on another piece of wood and then sat down opposite him. Looking directly at him, she spoke slowly as if she were feeling her way along.

"Elliott, something happened to me a few months ago that was the most momentous experience of my life."

Elliott waited, somewhat mystified. He had never seen Jessica so serious about anything.

But Jessica didn't immediately tell him what had happened to her. She reached over to an end table at her elbow and lifted a small, leather-bound book. Elliott's heart jumped like it was prodded with a hot iron. It was his mother's Bible.

"I see you recognize this," Jessica said with a little smile. "Do you remember when you saw it last?"

He remembered all right! He was fourteen and it was the day after his mother's funeral, just a short while before he was to leave for boarding school. He was standing in the hall, feeling lost, forlorn, and absolutely forsaken.

Jessica had come to him with his mother's Bible in her hands. "Elliott," she had said kindly, "your mother wanted me to give this to you after she was gone. She said to tell you that this Book directed her path through this life and gave her strength and wisdom and comfort. She wanted it to do the same for you."

He cringed a little now as he recalled his reaction. He had slammed the small book to the floor, then kicked it savagely across the room. "That's what I think of a God who took my mother away when I need her so bad!"

Jessica had calmly picked up the Bible, dusted it off, and said simply, "I know how you feel." She had not mentioned it again...yet she had kept the Bible all these years.

"You didn't want it then, I know," Jessica was saying, "but perhaps you feel differently now."

Elliott's voice was harsh and cold as he answered, "Why should I feel differently? The facts are still the same. God allowed my mother to suffer and die when she had every right to live and see her children grow up like other mothers. I don't need a God like that!"

Jessica looked full in Elliott's eyes for a long moment, her eyes full of sympathy and tender understanding. Elliott looked away, not wanting her to see the depth of his revulsion for anything religious.

"I felt the same way when your mother died," Jessica said gently. "I remember walking the floor and giving God a piece of my mind. Not that I was even convinced there was such a person as God."

Elliott looked up in surprise. He couldn't imagine her getting that emotional about anything.

"Your mother was a rare and wonderful human being," Jessica said. "I never had much love in my life—my mother died when I was born, and Father was not a loving person—much like Cyrus. But when your mother married my brother and came here to Coppercrest, we soon became very close and dear friends. She was sister, mother, and confidante to me, all rolled into one frail, beautiful, caring person."

Jessica was silent for a moment, and Elliott could see she was struggling with tears that threatened to fall. Choking them back, she went on. "W-when Ellen died, I felt like the light had gone out of the world for me. Ellen was my only real friend. I was absolutely devastated. And I blamed God for it, just as you did!"

She reached over and laid a soft hand on Elliott's arm. "Later, I realized I should have supported and comforted you when your mother died, but I couldn't see anything else at the moment but my own terrible grief.

"Weeks later—when I was tramping through a rain forest on the other side of the world, searching for a new variety of hummingbird, I suddenly saw the injustice I had done you. But it was too late, then. We could have comforted each other, but I was too self-centered to see that. Please forgive me, if you can, dear Elliott!"

"You made up for any oversight on your part many times over," Elliott said huskily. "You will never know how much it meant to me when you would call me from some distant city or drop in and take me to lunch or shopping. You were the only one who ever bothered. I knew you cared because you took some time for me."

"Not as much as I should have," Jessica said, "and much of what I did was purely selfish. I needed you more than you needed me. You were all I had left of my dearest friend, Ellen.

"But enough of that!" she said decisively. "What is done, is done, and it can't be undone. I didn't ask you here to cry on your shoulder but to tell you my wonderful, glorious news. I have met the Jesus your mother talked about!"

Elliott's dark eyes widened with incredulity. "You mean you've got religion?"

Jessica laughed softly. "No, I've not 'got religion.' I've got God's Son, Jesus Christ, in my life now."

Disappointment surged up inside Elliott. He had hoped Jessica had something of importance to tell him, and all she wanted to say was that she had turned into a religious fanatic.

Jessica's gruff laugh broke into his thoughts. "I can read your face like a book, Elliott Fleet, and you are very disappointed with your old aunt. Are you forgetting, young man, that your mother was a Christian, and she wasn't objectionable to you?"

"But–but Mother needed a strong belief in something to help

her through her years of weakness and illness," Elliott defended. "And she never pushed her religion off on anyone—not even me, as a child."

Jessica studied his face for a moment and then said slowly, "No, she didn't, but she told me once that she wished she had been able to introduce you to her Lord when you were small and not hardened toward God. She knew you were never treated fairly by your stepfather and half-brother and feared your pain was hardening you toward people and God."

"Aunt Jess, I don't want to offend you because you are a very special person to me," Elliott said gently, "but religion is one thing I don't discuss with anyone."

"I understand," Jessica said, "but I urge you to accept your mother's Bible. I've kept it all these years because she personally gave me the responsibility of delivering it to you. What you do with it is your business, but please take it."

Elliott took a long breath. He didn't even want to touch that Bible. Then he took hold of his emotions and scolded himself. The Bible was only a small, very old book. Nothing more, nothing less. It was his mother's wish that he have it—and he didn't wish to offend his aunt.

He reached out and took the book in his hand. It felt cool and leathery in his hand, just like any ordinary book, he discovered with relief. He slipped the Bible into his coat pocket.

"Now," Jessica said, typically changing the subject abruptly, "did you bring your mother's photographs?"

Elliott drew them out of his pocket and handed them to her.

"You wouldn't believe the commotion that went on here when these turned up missing after you had left for school," Jessica said softly.

"Why?" Elliott asked. "Mother gave them to me. Why would anyone else want them—and badly, too?"

"Cyrus thought Ellen hid a legal document behind one of the pictures," Jessica said, turning the pictures over and examining the backs of them.

"A legal document?" Elliott said in astonishment. "What kind of document?"

"I'm not sure," Jessica said slowly, "but it was a paper a lawyer had me witness before your mother and Cyrus married."

A tremor went through Elliott's body. "If you signed it, wouldn't you know what was in it?"

"The lawyer didn't enlighten me on its contents," Jessica said, "and neither did Cyrus. I was just called to witness Ellen's and Cyrus's signatures."

"And you think it's hidden behind one of these pictures! Let's look. I've got a knife in my pocket. It won't take a minute to get the backs off."

As he pried the cardboard back off the first photo, Elliott recalled how his mother had urged him to hide the photos and not to tell anyone he had them. He had taken them out to a special hiding place outdoors and retrieved them only a few minutes before he left for boarding school.

The first cardboard was off, but nothing was behind it. Elliott's heart was pounding like surf on the beach as he pried off the second cardboard backing. Again, there was nothing. Elliott attacked the third photo.

He yanked it off—and disappointment filled him.

"But it must be there!" Jessica cried. She took each piece of cardboard, turning it over and over, studying it carefully. "I was so sure it would be there," she said in a puzzled tone.

She looked up at Elliott and sighed, "I'm sorry I got you all excited for nothing. I still can hardly believe there is nothing hidden there. Has anyone had opportunity to steal the paper from you, Elliott?"

"I suppose so," Elliott said. "These sat on my bedside table all through boarding school and college and have traveled all over the world with me on my news trips. But no one has ever shown any interest whatever in them until now."

"None of the family ever visited you while you were in school or college?"

"No one except you."

"Did your mother ever tell you she had an important document that concerned you?"

"N–no," Elliott said slowly.

"Not even when she gave you these photographs?"

"No, she was trying to tell me something, but she died before she finished the sentence." His heart thumped. "You don't suppose she was trying to tell me about it then?"

"Can you remember the words she said?" Jessica asked.

"I remember everything she said that day," Elliott answered emphatically. "Her last words were: 'I have secured your—your....' I've often wondered what she had secured of mine."

"There's a good chance she was trying to tell you about it. I think that legal document had to do with you and that Ellen hid it. Cyrus obviously thought she hid it too," Jessica said. "I thought it might even be in the Bible, but I searched it carefully and it isn't there. Cyrus also searched it, I might add."

"When Cyrus had everyone searching for these pictures, didn't he tell anyone what he was looking for?"

Jessica shook her head. "My brother is a very secretive person and all he said was that Ellen had 'put away' a document that was vital to the company business. But since Cyrus always handled the Gypsy Blue business, I surmised it must have been the paper I put my signature on."

"And Mother never hinted what the document contained?"

"The only thing she ever said was that she had taken care of your future for you."

"Of course that could mean that she had persuaded Cyrus to finance my education," Elliott said. "Perhaps she made him sign a paper to that effect before she would marry him."

"I think it was more than that," Jessica said. "Even without finding the paper, he put you through school. It had to be something very important to Cyrus. If only we could find that document!"

7

When Elliott returned to his room, he looked through the open door into Steven's room and saw Marvin. The Barfield chauffeur was sitting near a lamp reading. He stepped to the door and spoke softly, "Marvin, is Steven asleep?"

The young man came quickly to his feet. Coming over to the door, he whispered, "Yes, at last. Miss Star asked me to stay with him until one of you returned."

"Would you mind staying with him for an hour or so more?" Elliott asked. "I really need to go downstairs for awhile."

"Sure, I'm just doing a little reading anyway."

Marvin stood with his book in his hand, and Elliott noticed that it was a textbook on writing. "You're interested in writing?" Elliott asked.

"Yes, sir, I'm taking a couple of classes down at the branch college."

"If you need any help, that's my field," Elliott said.

"Thank you, sir! That's really nice of you!" Marvin's deep blue eyes lighted with pleasure, and his white teeth flashed behind the heavy brown mustache and thick, clipped beard. One dark eyebrow lifted slightly as he grinned.

Elliott studied the chauffeur. The man was about five foot eight, with an athletic, whip-thin build, and his uniform was immaculate. The slim hand that held the book was tanned and strong-looking; the nails were clipped and clean.

"Where did you come from?" Elliott asked suddenly.

"From Maine, sir," Marvin answered. "I worked for a family

up there that knew your Aunt Jessica, and when they decided to go abroad for a year, they recommended me to Miss Barfield."

"So you are just working as a chauffeur until you get enough training to break into newspaper work?"

"Well, I wanted to start with newspaper reporting, but I would eventually like to write, mainly fiction," Marvin said. "Short stories and maybe a book. I'm especially interested in kids' picture books. I have a little drawing talent, I think."

"You aren't married, I take it?" Elliott asked.

He laughed self-consciously, "No."

"Keep it that way until you are established in your career," Elliott said emphatically. "News reporters don't make much at first."

"Thanks for the advice," Marvin said earnestly, "but it will be a long, long time before I have the training for newspaper work. And I'm happy here. I just want to do my job as well as I can. The pay is good, and I like driving and taking care of the cars."

Elliott nodded and left. When he entered the family room a few minutes later, he saw that Cyrus was there with Allyssa and Gentry, sitting in comfortable chairs watching a program. Cyrus nodded coldly as Gentry looked up and invited him to join them. Allyssa smiled a welcome and said, "We're glad you could join us."

As Elliott made himself comfortable, he saw they were looking at a National Geographic special. He waited until a commercial break came on and then spoke.

"I understand there has been some interest in my mother's photographs. Jessica seemed to think there is reason to believe Mother hid a legal document behind one of them."

Elliott saw his stepfather suddenly jerk around, alertness bright in his eyes. He continued, "I took the cardboard backs off, but Aunt Jess and I could find nothing behind the photographs. You're welcome to look at them, too, if you like."

"Let me see them," Cyrus said.

Elliott had not replaced the cardboard backs, so now he handed him the frames, photos, and pieces of cardboard backing in a small stack.

Cyrus examined each piece before handing them to Gentry, who expressed a desire to see them, too.

"As you can see, there is nothing hidden there," Elliott said after Cyrus had finished with them.

"Maybe you removed it long ago," Cyrus accused brusquely.

"What was in the document?" Elliott asked pointedly.

"If you found it, you would know," Cyrus said slowly.

"I believe that document had to do with me," Elliott said.

"Bosh!" Cyrus said. "I suppose Jessica has been filling you full of that nonsense! It was a business paper of concern to me only."

"Aunt Jessica said she witnessed a document that you and my mother had drawn up about two months before you and Mother married. I believe I have a right to know what that document contained. Mother was carrying me at that time, and anything she signed would affect me, her unborn son...and heir."

"What we signed was between your mother and me and is none of your business," Cyrus said coldly.

"It must have been an important document," Elliott said just as coldly. "I understand you had the servants and everyone searching everywhere for these photographs after Mother died because you thought she had hidden it there. If it did not concern me, why would you think Mother gave it to me?"

"How do I know your mother gave them to you? Maybe you just took them!"

"I'm sure you were very much aware that Mother called me to her room just a few minutes before she died," Elliott said harshly. "That was when she gave me the photographs—and told me they were mine. She told me to hide them and to tell no one I had them. I don't know what happened to the document, but Mother must have thought she was giving me more than three photographs—that would mean little to anyone but me."

During this discourse, Gentry and Allyssa had sat silently, but Elliott knew they were listening attentively.

A cunning look settled in Cyrus's eyes. "If your mother thought something was hidden behind the pictures, why didn't she tell you it was there?"

A slight smile played upon Elliott's lips. "She tried to tell me something, but she died before she finished."

"What did she say?" Cyrus demanded.

"She said, 'I have secured your—your...' and then she was unable to finish," Elliott said. He leaned toward his stepfather. "And I'm sure you know what she secured for me. What was it?"

Cyrus stared into Elliott's glaring eyes for a moment, then he let out a shrill bark of laughter. "I have no idea what you are talking about. You have a great deal of imagination. I wonder how much of what you write for your newspaper is fact and how much is your fertile imagination."

"I deal in facts, verifiable facts," Elliott said, gathering up his photographs from a table where they were now laying. "And—if there is a document somewhere that concerns me, I will find it! Goodnight, Stepfather. Goodnight, Allyssa...Gentry."

Elliott walked out, but not before his dark eyes swept over the three people in the room to see their reactions. Quick alarm showed clearly in Cyrus's eyes. Gentry and Allyssa were both watching him rather than Elliott. Then Allyssa turned warm blue-grey eyes toward Elliott and said earnestly, "Goodnight, Elliott—and good luck."

Elliott caught the quick frown on Gentry's face and heard him mutter something to Allyssa that didn't quite reach Elliott's ears.

8

As Elliott strode from the family room, he saw a flash of movement and a door closing quickly on his right. Like a cat, he sprinted across the room and grabbed the door knob. The door was locked! Someone had obviously been listening to his conversation with Cyrus! Someone who did not wish to be seen.

Maybe it was Tilda, he reasoned. The housekeeper was a sweet, motherly woman but she always did like to know what was going on. But if she had wanted to know what he had discussed with Cyrus, she could have asked Gentry. He was her son.

There were the day-servants, but the only other people he knew for sure were in the house in the evenings were Tilda, John, Aunt Jessica, Steven and the chauffeur.

Aunt Jess would probably have walked in openly and listened; Steven was asleep; John usually didn't come into the main part of the house at all, he recalled, unless sent for. And the chauffeur was with Steven—or was he?

Elliott rushed up the stairs and down the hall to Steven's room. Marvin was seated under the lamp, engrossed in his textbook. When Elliott came into the room, Marvin rose leisurely from his chair and spoke softly, "Back already?"

Elliott looked at him closely. Marvin looked calm and collected and was breathing normally—not like he would have been if he had sprinted upstairs to reach the room ahead of Elliott. So—the spy almost had to be Tilda.

Probably just curious, Elliott surmised, *and she naturally did not wish to be caught eavesdropping!*

He dismissed the incident from his mind, dismissed Marvin just as rapidly, and went to check on Steven. His bed was in a small alcove curtained off from the rest of the comfortable, large room.

Elliott drew back the curtain and in the dim light saw that Steven was sound asleep, curled up like a baby. He looked very small and defenseless. *He looks nothing like Austin*, Elliott thought with relief. *And let's hope he isn't like him in character, either.*

Elliott's mind drew painful memories back from the place Elliott thought he had buried them.

Austin was a sadist. Even as a small child he had delighted in hurting things: other children, animals, even his old nurse—though she idolized him and didn't realize he meant to hurt her when he pummeled her with his small fists or kicked her. He's just a little spoiled, she had rationalized to the household.

But Elliott knew better. He grew up with Austin and experienced his cruelty firsthand. At first, he had told his stepfather when Austin played mean tricks on him and others, but Cyrus would never believe his own precious son could do any wrong.

Ellen would scold Austin severely when she caught him in a wrong, but she was ill so much that she was seldom around him. His father never disciplined him in any way. Hurting animals and people must have given Austin a sense of power, Elliott reasoned now.

Elliott had soon learned to steer clear of Austin. But that often did not work either. Austin delighted in destroying or damaging things—sometimes costly and treasured items—and then telling his father that Elliott had done it. Then he would stand back and openly gloat in the punishment that Cyrus was always quick to administer to Elliott for any misdeed.

Elliott pushed the unpleasant thoughts away. Austin was

dead now and could no longer hurt or destroy. *I wonder*, he mused, *if that is why Lee killed Austin. Did he abuse her?*

Elliott closed the curtain around the bed, then checked Steven's door and windows to see that all was secure before going to his own room. There he checked his windows and locked the door that opened on the hall.

He was pleased to see his room had an outside entrance. Opening the door, he stepped out onto a small covered deck. The sweet odor of honeysuckle from vines in wooden tubs on either side of the door and running up on trellises filled his nostrils. He breathed deeply. This was an addition to the house since he had lived here.

He strolled out to the wooden parapet that surrounded the deck and looked down. Stone treads followed the side of the house to a small garden below, enclosed by a rock wall. A huge, yellow moon spilled soft, mellow light onto a small tree, a bed of flowers and a tiny patch of lawn.

A metal gate was set in the far side of the stone wall and Elliott—from his elevated position—could see a long, narrow flight of stone stairs curving steeply downward beyond it, a man-made canyon between stone walls.

As a child, these stone and concrete stairways that connected the lower terraces of houses to homes on higher levels on the steep hillsides had always fascinated him. He had probably climbed them all at one time or another when he was a boy. But this one he didn't remember. It would be interesting to see where it led in the daylight.

He returned to his room feeling more relaxed than he had since he arrived. He had forgotten what a unique place Bisbee was. People came from all over the country to explore its narrow, winding streets; its houses clinging to steep hillsides; its curious little shops and old buildings. Maybe he would enjoy his visit here, after all. Maybe he could take Steven and explore it all through his five-year-old eyes.

He had just taken off his shoes when a tap came at the door

and Tilda called urgently, "Mr. Barfield said could you come right down. Another letter just came from Lee. He's in his room."

When Elliott entered Cyrus's room a few minutes later, he saw him sitting close to the fire with a robe covering his legs. His silvered head lay wearily against the chairback. His thin hands held a sheet of paper torn from a spiral notebook.

Cyrus straightened up and handed the note to Elliott. "It's written to you this time."

The printed message—written with a black ballpoint pen—was short, as usual:

"Elliott, go back to your newspaper! I plan to have my son, and if you get in my way, you may never live to write another story!"

"She never signs the notes," Elliott said. "Do you suppose these could be prank notes? Everyone knows Lee escaped from prison. Maybe someone resents the wealthy Barfield family and wants to worry them."

"I guess anything is possible," Cyrus said, "but I wouldn't count on it. In my opinion, a person who would kill her husband is capable of anything."

"What reason did Lee give for killing Austin?" Elliott asked bluntly.

"What difference does it make?" Cyrus asked irritably.

"I would like to know as much as possible about Lee," Elliott said. "I want to know how she thinks, how she might act, and what she might do. So I need to know the reason she gave for killing her husband."

"She didn't admit to killing Austin. She said they had an argument, and she picked up a pipe wrench and threatened him. But she swore she never touched him. She claims he was still alive when she ran upstairs and left him."

"What was the argument about?"

"She said it was over Steven—and other things—and that he threatened her physically."

"Had Austin ever abused Lee?" Elliott asked.

"Of course not! What a question to ask about your dead half-brother."

"My half-brother loved to hurt people," Elliott said forcefully. "I figured he would graduate to wife-beating if he ever married."

Cyrus struggled to his feet, his face pale with anger, "I'll not have you talking about my dead son that way!"

"If you had disciplined your dead son when he was a boy, he might be alive today!" Elliott shouted.

The door was flung open and Gentry stood in the doorway. "What's going on here?"

Cyrus fell back in his chair, "Get Elliott out of here!"

"Don't bother. I'll not only get out of your room, I'll get out of your house," Elliott said angrily.

"G–get me a drink," Elliott heard Cyrus say as he marched from the bedroom.

"Well, that is that!" Elliott muttered as he charged up the stairs. "He won't let me stay now and I'm glad!"

As he let himself into his room, he was already beginning to feel better. "Maybe, I'll spend the rest of my vacation in San Diego, deep-sea fishing," he said with satisfaction.

Then he stopped short. He had put his mother's photographs back in their frames, but now they were out of the frames again—and what was left of the cardboard backs was scattered on the table and on the floor under it.

With pounding heart, he crossed swiftly to the table and picked up the three pictures. He sighed with relief. The photos—and frames—were unharmed. But each one of the photos' cardboard backing had been cut into tiny pieces!

9

Early the next morning, Elliott awoke to a soft tap on his door. Still half asleep, he climbed out of bed, grabbed a robe, and padded to the door in bare feet. When he opened it, there was no one there. Puzzled, Elliott stepped out into the hall and looked both ways but saw no one.

Stepping back into the dimness of the room, he glanced down and saw a white object on the dark carpet. He bent to pick it up and saw it was a small envelope. "What now?" he said aloud, "Another of Lee's little love notes?"

He pushed the door closed with his foot and turned on the light. Tearing open the envelope, he read the few words:

"Elliott, what you are looking for is in the post office, addressed to you. Call for it through General Delivery."

Elliott felt his heart race. Was this a prank? Well, he wouldn't leave town until he checked it out.

Elliott debated about getting dressed and going downtown before anyone else was up but felt he still had a responsibility to stay with Steven until he was relieved. *I suppose Cyrus has terminated me permanently,* he told himself wryly, *but I took on the job so I'll stay until Allyssa comes.*

He lay down and tried to go back to sleep, but his mind kept jumping to what was waiting for him in the post office.

Finally, he got up, showered, and dressed for the day. It was only six o'clock. He could find nothing in the room to read and there was no television. Suddenly, he remembered his mother's little Bible, still in his jacket pocket.

He went to his closet and felt around in the inside pocket of the suit coat he had worn the night before. A pang of dismay stabbed through him. The Bible wasn't there!

"This is ridiculous!" he said aloud. "Of course it's there."

He took the coat off the hanger and felt in all the pockets. But the Bible was gone! Thoroughly disturbed now, he looked his clothes over carefully. Usually he was pretty careless about what he wore. Maybe he had worn the other tan suit that was close to the same color, he reasoned. When the Bible wasn't in it, he looked in his blue suit which he knew he had not worn. But the Bible had vanished!

Elliott spent the next half hour pacing his room and the small deck outside, muttering to himself in anger and dismay. What was going on in this house? Who would want to steal his mother's Bible?

He shuddered as a thought took root in his mind. What if that "someone" also cut his mother's Bible into little pieces, searching for whatever he was searching for? The thought was inexplicably devastating. Now that he had accepted the idea of possessing his mother's Bible, its loss made him feel like he had been deprived of something infinitely precious.

He was relieved when Allyssa knocked at his door at seven-thirty. Excusing himself courteously but quickly, Elliott left the house without seeing anyone else.

At the post office, he had to wait a few minutes until the window opened. But at last he had a long white envelope in his hand, addressed in block letters to Mr. Elliott Fleet.

Elliott moved to a side window and ripped open the envelope.

It contained a letter, but he skimmed the other, official-looking sheet of paper first. His eyes widened, and he seemed to have trouble breathing as he stopped to read the document and then re-read it carefully and thoroughly.

The essence of the full-page legal document was that Ellen Fleet had been given a quarter interest in Blue Gypsy Enterprises for an investment of one hundred thousand dollars in the company. In the event of her death, the child that she was carrying on the date recorded would receive her quarter of the company.

Cyrus Barfield was named as the child's guardian until the child became twenty-one, at which time the child would become a partner in Blue Gypsy Enterprises.

Elliott read the document through a third time, his heart accelerating like a runaway train. Then he lowered the paper and stared out the window. He owned a quarter of Gypsy Blue Enterprises! No wonder Cyrus had searched so hard for this paper! The old scoundrel! *He denied me the inheritance that should have come to me at Mother's death!*

Suddenly, he remembered the letter that was with the legal document. He opened it and received another shock. It was signed Lee Barfield!

"Elliott,

"Your brother, Austin, saw your mother hide this document inside one of the photographs that she gave you just before she died. Austin stole it before she gave you the pictures.

"At our wedding reception, Austin had a little too much champagne, and he bragged about stealing it and told me where it was hidden.

"After I broke out of prison, I looked and was greatly surprised to find it still there.

"I am helping you. I desperately need your help. I did not kill my husband. There were times, I'll admit, when he knocked me around and bullied me that I felt like murdering him, though.

"Would you try to find out who did kill Austin? I have a friend who will hire a good lawyer for me, but we must first come up with some sound evidence that I did not murder Austin.

"Please *help me!*"

                                        Lee Barfield

10

Before Elliott went back to Coppercrest, he made a copy of the document and put the original in a safety deposit box at the bank.

Then he had breakfast in a small cafe in town and arrived back at Coppercrest about ten. Even before he had his car parked, Tilda was out on the wide veranda waiting for him.

Her face anxious, Tilda came down the steps to meet him. "Elliott, Mr. Barfield is almost beside himself. He thinks you left, even though I told him your clothes were still in your room. He won't eat or take his medication or anything!"

"I thought he would have had you throw my clothes out in the street instead of wanting me to stay," Elliott said in surprise. "He was mighty upset with me last night."

"Please go right to him," Tilda urged. "He's in his room. And make him take his medication, please."

"That'll be the day when I can make Cyrus Barfield do anything," Elliott retorted. "But I'll go see if he throws me out."

Gentry answered the door when Elliott knocked. He was dressed for work.

Cyrus was in a wheelchair, and he looked a little wild. His hair had not been combed, and he was still in his pajamas and robe.

"What do you mean running off like that?" he demanded as soon as Elliott crossed the threshold.

Elliott walked slowly to his stepfather's wheelchair before he said calmly, "I didn't know I had to ask your permission whenever I leave the house."

"I thought you left," Cyrus said plaintively.

"I supposed you would want me to leave, after we quarreled last night."

"No–no, I just got a little upset last night," Cyrus said in a calmer voice. He turned to Gentry, "I want to speak to Elliott alone."

"Perhaps I should stay," Gentry said persuasively. "I don't want you getting all upset again."

"What I have to discuss with my stepson is none of your affair," Cyrus said crossly.

"But, sir, getting upset is bad for your health."

"Arguing with you is harder on my health than anything right now!"

"Don't you think you had better take your medicine before I go?"

"No! Get out of here before I really do lose my temper!"

A dull flush rose in Gentry's face, but he turned abruptly and left the room.

"That's real diplomacy," Elliott muttered to himself, "same old Cyrus!"

"What? What did you say?" Cyrus demanded.

"Nothing—nothing of importance," Elliott replied. He hadn't realized he had spoken his thoughts aloud. "Now, what was it you wished to see me about?"

"First of all, I hired you to go everywhere with Steven, and yet this morning I had to send John with him and Allyssa to get Steven's immunization vaccinations!"

Elliott spoke as patiently as he could; his blood was beginning to boil at the words of the tyrannical old man. "I didn't leave this morning until Allyssa came up. Then I had very important business to attend to that I felt couldn't wait."

He hesitated and then looked Cyrus full in the eyes. "Besides, I figured you had given me my walking papers last night when you ordered me out of the room."

"Well, I didn't! I just won't stand for any bad-mouthing of my dead son!"

Nor when he was alive either, even when he deserved a good thrashing, Elliott thought. But he didn't speak his mind.

Cyrus eyed Elliott speculatively for a moment, then said slowly, "I have a proposition to make you. I'm not well and Steven needs a guardian. I'll make it worthwhile to you. Would you take on that responsibility?"

As stunned as he was, Elliott didn't need to think about that proposition! "Absolutely not! I don't want to be tied down in this hick town—or to a kid! I'm a roving reporter. I like it, and I don't plan to change my vocation for anybody!"

"Don't be so quick to turn it down," Cyrus said. "I could make it very much worth your while—financially, I mean."

"Sorry, I'm not interested!"

"What if I offer you a ten percent share in Gypsy Blue Enterprises? And offered you a good salary, besides—as vice-president of the company?"

Elliott stared at his stepfather in astonishment. Cyrus was offering him a vice-presidency in his precious company! To the stepson he had always treated like trash! But he shook his head adamantly. "Gentry would be far more capable as both a guardian and vice-president. I know nothing about your business, and he's worked for you ever since college; he knows the business as well as you do. He knows Steven, and Steven knows him. And if anybody's earned that place, it's Gentry. He's the logical man for the job."

Cyrus's eyes went cold and hard. "I no longer trust Gentry. He—he keeps pressuring me to make him Steven's guardian—and for more authority in managing Gypsy Blue Enterprises."

Raw fear showed plainly in Cyrus's eyes, and his words sank to almost a whisper. "He has never liked Steven, just as he never liked Austin, even though he hides it under a veneer of geniality!"

Cyrus stared off into space for a moment, "But I have seen the look on his face sometimes, as he looks at my grandson. Just like he used to look at Austin—when he thought I wasn't noticing."

"Surely you are imagining things," Elliott interposed. "Gentry wouldn't..."

But Cyrus seemed not to hear Elliott's protest as he went on. "His eyes get a sly, mean look to them, like a hawk's trained on a fat pigeon."

"If you never trusted him, why did you make him your manager?"

"Gentry has exceptional management ability. I thought Austin and I could use him, while keeping his ambitions under control. But now Austin is dead, and my body has betrayed me!" Cyrus finished bitterly.

"What are Gentry's ambitions?" Elliott asked gently. He wondered if the old man's sickness, his greed, and the loss of his son was making him paranoid.

"To be the master of Gypsy Blue Enterprises, of course! To take my place!"

A perverse excitement kindled in Cyrus's eyes as he leaned toward Elliott and said with a conspiratorial chuckle, "But together we can circumvent his plans. *You* will learn the business and take over the reins when I am no longer able. When Steven is old enough, he will be the president and you will still be the vice-president."

When Elliott said nothing, Cyrus spoke in an exasperated voice, "Don't you see? With a one-tenth share of the company stock, a home at Coppercrest, plus a handsome salary, you will be set for life!"

"You are forgetting one thing, Stepfather," Elliott said dryly. "I am already owner of one-fourth of the shares of Gypsy Blue Enterprises—as my mother's heir."

Cyrus's pale face turned as white and lifeless as the marble of his massive fireplace. For a moment he stared at Elliott through stricken eyes. "You–you know," he said in a choked voice. He swallowed convulsively. Then, suddenly, he slumped down in the chair, closed his eyes wearily and laid his shrunken, silver head against the chair back. His breathing became erratic and shallow.

Alarmed, Elliott got quickly to his feet. "Are you all right? Where's your medicine?"

"On the tray." Cyrus raised a trembling hand to point. "O–over there."

When Elliott brought the whole tray over—since it held several prescription bottles—Cyrus touched one. "That one. Put one under my tongue."

After Elliott had placed the medication in the old man's mouth, he asked quickly, "Shouldn't we call your doctor or get you to the hospital?"

"No! I'll be all right in a few minutes," Cyrus said as decisively as he could while holding the pill under his tongue.

For a few minutes Cyrus lay still and silent in the wheelchair. As Elliott paced the floor, while keeping a close eye on Cyrus, he was surprised to feel a stirring of pity. The gaunt figure, held prisoner in the large chair, had been reduced to only a shadow of the tall, grim, unloving man who had put such fear, misery, and anger in his heart as a child.

Cyrus raised his head after a few minutes and said faintly, "Maybe I had better take my other medicine, too. Get me a capsule from that blue bottle and two from the smallest bottle."

Elliott held the glass of water that was also on the tray for his stepfather as he swallowed the medicine. "I'll have to eat a little of that toast," Cyrus said with a grimace. "The medications are supposed to be taken with food and water."

Elliott brought his breakfast tray and was surprised to hear Cyrus thank him—not a very hearty one—but a thanks, nevertheless.

"I can get some breakfast sent over for you," he offered after he had slowly eaten a few bites of toast.

"No thanks," Elliott said. "I ate before I came back to Coppercrest."

Cyrus kept his eyes on his plate as he chewed and swallowed a few more bites of toast. Then he looked at Elliott. "The paper was hidden behind one of your mother's pictures, after all. Why did you give us that song and dance about it not being there?"

"It wasn't hidden there," Elliott said.

"Where, then? Not in Ellen's Bible. I searched it myself."

"No, not there either," Elliott said.

"Where then?" Cyrus was regaining his old, demanding tone.

"For the moment, let's just say that I came into possession of it."

"How do I know you really have it?"

For an answer, Elliott brought the paper out and handed it to Cyrus.

"This is only a copy," he stated.

"I assure you, I have the original," Elliott said. "In a safe place."

Cyrus handed the paper back, and Elliott saw his hand shake like an aspen leaf.

Cyrus pushed the tray away suddenly. "That's all that I can eat. Please move it away from me. The sight and smell of food nauseates me."

I imagine the food is not what nauseated you, Elliott thought. *It's because I am now a part owner of your precious Gypsy Blue Enterprises!* But, strangely, he didn't feel the triumph he would have expected from turning the tables on his stepfather.

"Okay," Cyrus said heavily, "so you are part owner of my business. It seems that would give you real initiative to become Steven's guardian—to protect your own interests. The offer still holds: you can live at Coppercrest, learn the business, and draw the salary of vice-president."

"No, thanks! If you don't trust Gentry, then have him train someone else and boot Gentry out when you no longer need him. Isn't that what you plan to do? It doesn't matter to you that he has given his whole life being useful to you!" For some irrational reason, Elliott was angry again. "He should be your vice-president—until your whim changes!"

Cyrus stared at him for a minute and then laughed—a sharp bark of derision. "Are you actually taking up for Gentry? I didn't think you even liked him when you were growing up together."

"I didn't, but that is beside the point. He has served you loyally. And you would give him the boot as if he had never grown up in this house, slaving for you!"

"He was paid well," Cyrus said belligerently.

Elliott studied Cyrus for a moment, then locked eyes with him. He said bitterly, "But that isn't as bad as what you did to me, is it? You treated me worse than a servant, putting cane marks on my body when I was barely able to walk!

"And when you paid for my schooling, you made me feel like a beggar who should be grateful to you! And all the time the money came out of my inheritance that you conveniently never told me about!"

Fire leaped into Cyrus's eyes and he raised his voice, "Gypsy Blue Enterprises is mine! Ellen had no right to demand I make over a quarter of my company to her for a measly one hundred thousand dollars!"

"Why did you do it then, Cyrus Barfield?" Elliott's anger matched Cyrus's.

"I needed money!" Cyrus shouted. "The ore was running out in the mine, and the banks wouldn't loan me any more money. I *had* to have more money to strike out in other directions—to save Gypsy Blue Enterprises!"

"Where did Mother get one hundred thousand dollars?"

"Your mother inherited your father's estate when he died in the Korean war."

"And you knew about her money and set out to marry her—to get her money?" Elliott demanded.

"I would never have married her if she had not been from a good family, even for the money," Cyrus said stiffly.

Elliott's voice softened. "And Mother married you because she wasn't well and wanted someone to care for her unborn child. She married for love of me, and you married for greed!"

Suddenly he chuckled. "But the delicate lady outwitted you, Cyrus, didn't she? She made you sign an agreement that you would make her a partner, in order to protect her child. I suppose you only agreed because you thought you could destroy the paper after you were married and not have to fulfill your agreement."

"The–the little trickster hid it and would never reveal where it was hidden," Cyrus said fiercely.

"Well, bully for her!"

Cyrus glared at Elliott but didn't reply.

"Is that why you hated me?" Elliott asked. "Why you abused and humiliated me when I was growing up? I could never please you, no matter what I did!"

Sudden rage flamed in Cyrus's eyes. "She always loved him! Even kept pictures of him in her chest of drawers!"

"Loved who?" Elliott asked. "You mean my father? Mother loved him and never you?"

"Yes, she even wanted to talk to me about him. Gerald, the hero pilot!"

"You were jealous of a dead man!"

"Yes! Only he was never dead to your mother! Even after I tore up all the pictures of him I could get my hands on, Ellen still loved him. I know she did because she talked to you about him!"

"Cyrus, you are a stupid man," Elliott said acidly. "Mother only wanted me to know my father. If you had been the loving husband you should have been, you would have won my mother's love. If she retreated into a half-dream world where her first husband was the king of her heart, it was only because you drove her from you with your jealousy and hatefulness."

Cyrus turned his head away and said stubbornly, "It wouldn't have mattered what I did. She would never have loved me."

"You weren't—and aren't—a lovable person," Elliott said brutally. "But you didn't answer my question. Why did you hate me? Because I was the son of the woman who refused to love you?"

"You looked like your father! That's why Ellen loved you better even than Austin—*my* son! You looked like her hero husband. And what about me?" he said bitterly. "I couldn't forget for a moment that Ellen still loved Gerald when you walked about my house looking more like him every day!"

"So you took out your spite on a bewildered little kid because he looked like someone you hated! You are the most despicable man who ever lived!" Elliott lashed out, quickly getting to his feet. "The very air around you is contaminated!"

He was nearly to the door when Cyrus raged at him, "If you leave this house, I'll fight your claim to Gypsy Blue Enterprises in every court in the land!"

Elliott's laugh was harsh and derisive, but his words were soft and deadly. "Oh, I'm not leaving! I've decided to stay at Coppercrest for awhile. It should be interesting for both of us—*partner!*"

11

When Elliott reached the door, he realized that Gentry had left it open a few inches. And as he stepped out into the wide hall, he saw why. Gentry was standing near the door, obviously listening.

Also in the hall were Allyssa, Steven, and Marvin. Plainly, they had just returned from the doctor's office and had been arrested by the argument raging between Elliott and Cyrus.

From the corner of his eye Elliott glimpsed movement down the hall the other way and quickly turned his head. Standing in a doorway was Tilda. Well, no secrets here!

Gentry made no pretense about his eavesdropping but took a step backward and said softly, "So! The goose has outfoxed the fox! You are now a quarter owner of Gypsy Blue Enterprises. Do we call you 'boss' too?"

Elliott's dark eyes looked directly into Gentry's green ones. Was there sarcasm in his words? He could read nothing from the bland, innocent expression on Gentry's face.

"I'm still just a newsman," Elliott said slowly. "But I do plan to stay around until Steven's mother is found. I made a commitment and plan to keep it."

Allyssa came forward and extended a cool, soft hand. "Congratulations, Elliott! We couldn't help but hear. I hope everything works out well for you, as part owner of Gypsy Blue Enterprises." Her blue-grey eyes were warm and friendly.

Elliott felt a tightening in his throat, and his heart was

pumping much more strongly than it should.

As Elliott took Allyssa's slim hand into his own, he glimpsed Steven beyond her, sitting on the floor playing with a car, uninterested in the drama unfolding about him. But one couldn't say that for Marvin, Elliott thought. His dark blue eyes were intent and watchful.

When Marvin noticed Elliott's eyes were on him, he quickly dropped his head but didn't move away.

"Thanks," Elliott said as his eyes came back to Allyssa.

"I'm curious," Allyssa said as she smiled up at him. "Where was that legal document hidden? In your mother's photos, after all?"

"No," Elliott said. "A friend found it and gave it to me."

"*Who* gave it to you?" a new voice spoke up and Elliott saw Jessica standing nearby.

Elliott's keen eyes swept over the whole group. Tilda had moved from the doorway and now stood close, too. Every eye was on him. Elliott decided to drop his bomb. "Lee Barfield gave it to me," he said.

Every face showed shock—even unbelief registered on Gentry's—except one. A faint smile tugged at Marvin's lips and his left eyebrow lifted slightly. The chauffeur's smile was fleeting and a careful indifference replaced it.

"You've got to be kidding!" Gentry's exclamation jerked Elliott's attention back to the others. "The police and everyone are looking for Lee!"

"You mean you saw Lee?" Tilda asked incredulously.

"No," Elliott said. "She wrote me a letter and told me I would find my inheritance paper at the post office. And I did!"

"Have you told the police? They will want to see the letter," Gentry said. "You aren't forgetting you were hired to protect Steven from that woman, are you?"

Ignoring Gentry's questions, Elliott said musingly, "I'm beginning to wonder if Lee really killed Austin. She declares she didn't."

"Of course she did!" Tilda exclaimed. "She was found guilty and sent to prison!"

"But sometimes juries make mistakes," Elliott said seriously. "And I hope to find out if this jury did."

"So you think you can find evidence four years later that the police couldn't find when the case was fresh?" Gentry said derisively.

"Well, I hope you can!" Jessica said. "Lee was somewhat of a scatterbrain but I never could imagine her killing anyone."

"Is there a picture of Lee around?" Elliott asked. "I really can't recall her appearance very well."

"I have a wedding picture," Tilda offered. Her face took on a stern look. "But I think she killed that poor boy and left little Steven the same as an orphan."

"Thanks, Tilda, could you get it for me? Does anyone else have any pictures?"

"Gentry is always taking videos," Allyssa volunteered. "He even carries a camcorder in his car." She turned to Gentry, "Don't I recall a cassette of Austin's and Lee's wedding and even some of their family after Steven was born?"

"Yeah, sure," Gentry said without enthusiasm. "The videos are in the family room. I'll get them for you, later, if you'd like."

"If it's possible, I'd like to see them now," Elliott said. "If you're busy, I can find them. Just tell me where they are."

"I guess I can take the time to find them," Gentry said grudgingly. "Then I had better get to work before the boss fires me."

Elliott saw that Marvin had quietly taken Steven's hand and was leading him up the stairs to his room. His eyes narrowed as he stared at the man's retreating back. He wished he knew what it was that bothered him about the quiet chauffeur.

12

As Elliott watched Gentry searching for the videos in a handsome cassette cabinet, Tilda came into the room and handed Elliott a large photograph of Austin's and Lee's wedding party.

"You can leave it in here when you get through with it," she said and left.

Elliott scarcely glanced at Austin's well-remembered, handsome face. He had had enough of his half-brother to last him a lifetime. Not even Austin's death could change his feelings of bitterness toward him.

He hadn't paid a great deal of attention to Austin's bride the one time he had seen her—at the wedding. He recalled, now, as he studied her face in the photo that he had been somewhat amazed when he saw her that Austin hadn't picked a beautiful woman. Girls had always been attracted to the good-looking heir to the Gypsy Blue fortune. Austin could have had his pick—or so Elliott had reasoned at the time.

Now he gazed at Lee's picture with real interest. Tall and slightly plump, with a pretty face, she looked softly pink and white. Like a white rabbit, he thought. He wondered again if Austin had abused her. She certainly didn't look as if she would have the gumption or nerve to stand up for herself—or kill anyone. However, if even a soft, helpless girl was pushed too far....

"Here they are," Gentry said. "And there's the VCR. Do you know how to operate one?" At Elliott's nod, he said, "Good, I'll go now." He started for the door, then turned back with a frown on his face. "I hope you aren't going to keep the old man upset all the time. He *is* far from well, you know." Gentry turned on his heel and strode out of the room.

For the next hour Elliott sat back and watched as the videos unfolded: first, the wedding; then, pictures of Coppercrest gatherings, parties, and other events with Gentry's mother and father and others, and often scenes of Austin and Lee. There was even one of Lee, in maternity clothes, at a baby shower. Her body had been large and bulky so it must have been shortly before the baby was born. Then there was one of her and the new baby in the hospital with Austin standing proudly behind her.

In the next footage, Elliott saw that Lee had lost little, if any, of the weight she had gained with her baby. Suddenly a scene slid into view that captivated Elliott. Gentry had caught an unguarded moment, out on the patio of Coppercrest. The expression on Lee's face was what arrested Elliott's attention. It was somehow appealing and even bewitching. Maybe he was seeing for the first time what might have drawn Austin to his wife.

Elliott rewound the tape so he could see that part again. Lee was laughing up into Austin's face, and one eyebrow slid up in a cocky quirk. Her face and eyes literally glowed with love. Austin was grinning at her. For a second, Elliott felt envy swell up inside him. It would be heavenly to have a girl look at you like that. Elliott suddenly felt the scene was too intimate for a prying camera to record and set the film in motion again.

One fact began to emerge clearly in Elliott's mind as the scenes unfolded before his eyes. Lee was a smiling, happy girl at her wedding but a strained look slipped over her in succeeding pictures, even when she was smiling. Only in the intimate scene and in the picture at the hospital with her baby did she really look radiantly and joyfully happy again.

In the last few scenes in which Lee appeared, always now with her baby, the strain and unhappiness were back and visibly intensified. In the last one there was almost a desperation in her eyes, Elliott felt. Again he wondered: Had Austin verbally or even physically abused his wife?

When he chose to be, Austin had been cruel and vindictive. He would cut cruelly with his words, but he could also hurt and wound intentionally with his hands or whatever lay at hand. Elliott had not only experienced it, he had seen him treat others shamefully—and seemingly with no remorse or conscience.

His hand moved to the back of his neck where a deep scar made by Austin still remained. Elliott had been eight and Austin seven. Elliott remembered the incident vividly.

Austin had gone into a rage because José, a young man who worked in their garden, did not want to give or sell Austin a piece of turquoise that he carried in his pocket as a good luck piece.

Austin had grabbed a hoe and attacked the young gardener with it. Elliott had yelled at Austin to stop, and Austin had turned on him, striking him on the neck with the sharp hoe. When he saw blood pouring from the wound, Austin had fled to the house and told his father that Elliott had threatened him with the hoe when he hadn't done anything. According to Austin's story, they had wrestled for the hoe and in the scuffle, Elliott had been hurt.

Elliott could still feel the hopeless sense of betrayal that had overwhelmed him twenty years ago when Cyrus had believed Austin, in spite of the fact that José, the young Mexican man, corroborated Elliott's version. After Elliott's wound had been sewn up at the hospital, he was banished to his room for a week and was not allowed to see anyone, even his mother.

When his punishment was over, Elliott discovered that José had been fired. He was accused of stealing the turquoise from Austin, who said he got it out of the family mine. Austin had had the turquoise polished, and he had carried it triumphantly on a chain around his neck until he grew tired of it after a few months and discarded it.

The pictures had ended while Elliott had been busy with his bitter memories. He rewound the tape to the scene of Lee in the hospital with her new baby and started it again. Suddenly, as the film again came to the intimate scene with Lee and Austin, something jumped out at Elliott. With his heart pounding, he rewound the tape and ran it again.

There! Elliott had been so absorbed with Lee's expression of love before that he had only vaguely noted the rest of her face. She was laughing, and the camera had caught a close-up of her face. As her lips curved into a smile, her left eyebrow lifted cockily.

Elliott's heart was pounding. The lifted eyebrow when Marvin smiled was what had made him look familiar! The strange little facial quirk was the one thing his mind had unconsciously recorded about Lee's face during the wedding and the reception afterward.

Did it mean something? Were the two related? Brother and sister, maybe?

Elliott rewound the tape again to where Lee was smiling at Austin. He stopped the tape and stared at the close-up of Lee's face, then ran it a tiny bit farther where he could see her full form and stopped it.

Somewhat disappointed, Elliott could see no resemblance in her form or face to Marvin—except the cock to her left eyebrow. His was on the left, too.

He studied Lee. They were about the same height, he decided, but Lee was plump and Marvin was thin as a willow switch. Her hair was a soft pale brown and his was a chestnut brown. Her eyes were a golden, copper-flecked hazel; Marvin's were dark blue. And, of course there was Marvin's dark, heavy beard.

Suddenly, a slightly amused voice spoke behind him, causing him to start.

"My, my! I didn't know you were such a fan of Lee's. I know you have been staring at her picture for at least five minutes!"

"Aunt Jess," Elliott said, "I was just doing a little speculating. Have you seen Lee since she was sent to prison?"

"You mean did I visit her in prison? No, I didn't, to my shame," Jess said quickly. "Why?"

"Oh—nothing. Just thinking. Sit down, if you can spare a minute." As she sat down, she was still looking at him with penetrating, questioning eyes.

Elliott asked abruptly, "How well do you know Marvin Maxell?" When she didn't answer immediately, he prompted gently, "You were the one who recommended him, I understand."

"Yes—yes, I was. But I didn't really know him at all. Cyrus was going to retire old Jim Parker, and a friend of mine recommended Marvin. He has proved a good choice, I might add," Jessica said, somewhat defensively.

"I don't doubt that," Elliott hastened to assure her. "He seems a very conscientious young man."

"What has Marvin to do with Lee?"

Elliott didn't answer right away but stood up and walked to the VCR to put away Gentry's equipment. Without turning around, he asked after a moment, "You knew Lee. Do you honestly believe she killed Austin?"

He swung around abruptly to watch her face as she answered without hesitation, "No, I do not! Lee Barfield couldn't hurt a fly!"

"Who do you think did kill him, then?"

"I could have killed him myself—with my bare hands—many times," Jessica spat. "And most of the people who knew him felt the same way, I'm sure! He was a sadistic, pompous, spoiled brat—in a handsome mature body!"

"Maybe Lee felt that way, too," Elliott said softly. A small smile tugged at his lips at Jessica's forcefulness. "Maybe she was a battered wife."

"I'm sure she was! Though she would never admit it to me! Several times she had a bruised face and once even a broken arm, but she always declared she was clumsy and had fallen."

"Maybe she really was a klutz?"

"Don't you believe it! That girl was a little overweight but she was as well-coordinated as an athlete. I've played tennis with her. I'm good and she beat me nearly every time! No, there was nothing klutzy about Lee Barfield!"

"Does she have any brothers—or sisters?"

"No, she didn't. And her parents were killed in a heli-skiing accident in Canada."

"Lee wasn't the kind of girl I would have expected Austin to marry," Elliott said. "A sophisticated, society belle was more his kind."

"What about a girl from an elite family—and the only heir to a fortune? Plus a sweet, innocent girl—raised in a girls' school—who could be wrapped around one's little finger? Austin's little finger? That girl loved Austin with all her soul, and he treated her like dirt from the day they were married!"

Elliott chuckled. "At least she has one loyal supporter." He locked eyes with Jessica in a penetrating stare and said softly but bluntly, "Did you help Lee escape?"

"No, I didn't, but if I had known how to go about it, I would have!"

"There was no way you could help her at the trial?"

Jessica shook her head. "I wasn't here when Austin was killed. The only thing I could do for her was stand up for her as a character witness. And I did—with Cyrus and all the others of this house looking holes through me!"

She paused. "No, that's not correct. Your old nurse, Sarah, and her husband, Jim, who was the old chauffeur for years, were intensely loyal—and outspoken about it. I think that is why Cyrus retired them—on a very small salary, I might add—after all their years of service to this family!"

"And I imagine you supplement it," Elliott said with a grin.

Jessica laughed lightly and patted Elliott's hand. "You know me well, don't you?" Then she sobered. "You will try to help clear Lee, won't you?"

Elliott thought for a moment, then spoke carefully. "I'm going to do my best to find out the truth, Aunt Jess. But I don't know if my efforts will do any good. The case is four years old, and the police have fully investigated, I'm sure."

"The police!" Jessica snorted scornfully. "They wouldn't have dared come up with any information except what would convict Lee. Cyrus was convinced she had killed his precious son and that was that!"

"Do you think Lee would harm Steven? Cyrus seems to be afraid she might—because of the notes."

"I don't think Lee is sending those notes," Jessica declared.

"Then who is?"

"I don't want to make accusations," Jessica said, lowering her voice. "But it wouldn't hurt to keep your eyes on Gentry. He loves Gypsy Blue Enterprises as much as Cyrus! That cursed business should have been named Deadly Gypsy Blue! The love of her turned both my father and brother into uncaring robots. They didn't own Gypsy Blue, she owned them!"

"And did Austin share this love for Gypsy Blue?"

"If he loved anything it was Gypsy Blue. He liked to be told he was going to own her one day."

"It sounds like the Gypsy Blue is a pretty lethal lady all right," Elliott said thoughtfully. "Maybe we can save Steven from her deadly charms if we start right now."

A pang shot through him. What was he saying! He didn't want to stay here! Coppercrest and Gypsy Blue had not been kind to him. Why should he try to save the heir of Gypsy Blue Enterprises? Steven was Austin's son. What if he grew up to be just like him? A shudder ran through him. Perhaps he *could* keep that from happening, but he didn't want to fall for the siren call of the Gypsy Blue. And he certainly did not want to live in Bisbee again. Not ever!

13

The door opened suddenly as Allyssa swept into the room. Her words included Jessica, but her smile was for Elliott.

"I hope I'm not interrupting anything?"

"No, come on in." Elliott, who prided himself on a cool, unperturbed demeanor, realized his voice betrayed his eagerness for her presence.

Allyssa advanced into the room. "Elliott, would you like to take lunch with Steven and me? Marvin quite often gives me a break at mealtimes by lunching with Steven. But today he is taking Mr. Barfield into town for his doctor's appointment. I thought it would be a good opportunity for you and Steven to get better acquainted—and I would enjoy it, too." Her smile and words were warm.

"Thanks, I'd love to," Elliott responded quickly, then wondered why a mere lunch invitation made him so happy.

"Good! We'll expect you in about thirty minutes." The tantalizing fragrance of her perfume lingered after she had gone.

"Well," Jessica said dryly, "I fear someone else will be less than delighted that you are lunching with his girl, even if Steven is present."

Elliott turned back to his aunt. "*Is* Allyssa Gentry's girlfriend?"

"Well, they aren't engaged—that I know of—but they have certainly been going out regularly. And Gentry is quite possessive about her for it not to be serious—at least with him."

"Well, she isn't wearing his ring," Elliott said. "And besides, this is just a little informal lunch. No big deal."

"It may be a big deal with Gentry," Jessica said dryly. "I imagine that diamond necklace, earrings, and jeweled watch he gave Allyssa set him back a bundle. And she accepted them, so their relationship must not be too casual."

Elliott whistled. "Well, perhaps it is more serious than I thought. However, I still don't think he should object to our lunching together informally."

"Gentry could be a formidable enemy," Jessica said slowly. "I wouldn't like to see you get crossed up with him. After all, you are my favorite nephew."

Elliott reached out and gave Jessica a quick hug, then said lightly, "I can take care of myself, but I'm not out to steal Gentry's girl. I'm the confirmed bachelor, remember?" But even as the words left his mouth, he wondered if he really was. None of the girls he had dated had ever attracted him strongly—not like this golden girl, Allyssa Star.

Small and shapely, her hair falling over her shoulders in shimmering waves of gold, the grey-blue eyes that changed color with the colors she was wearing, Allyssa was extremely pleasant to the eyes. But it wasn't just her physical attractiveness that drew him. Her friendliness and forthrightness appealed to him. Was he getting lonesome after all and subconsciously looking for that one special girl?

"I'd better get back to my work," Jessica said abruptly. Elliott knew she meant the workroom next to her suite where she made drawings and wrote about her research on hummingbirds.

"Just a minute, Aunt Jess," Elliott laid a restraining hand on her arm. "I need some more information. Would you tell me what happened when Austin was killed?"

"I have only the accounts of those who were here," Jessica said. "Remember, I wasn't at Coppercrest when it happened."

"I know, but I never even read a newspaper account of it, so

I would like to know how the story was reported."

Jessica sat back down, and Elliott sat opposite her as she began. "Austin and Lee were heard quarreling—down in that tiny little garden below your room. Then Lee ran upstairs to the room you have now. That was her room then and the nursery was next door—where Steven still sleeps.

"Tilda went out the side door and saw Austin lying on that little patch of lawn. He was dead."

"How was he killed?"

"With a heavy pipe wrench, struck on the head from behind."

"With a pipe wrench? What was a wrench doing in that little garden?"

"John had been using the wrench, he said, to work on some pipes under the house. He had gone to supper and left the wrench there because he planned to finish the work later. Only his and Lee's fingerprints were on the wrench. John had an alibi; Lee didn't. John was having supper with Tilda when it happened."

"It sounds like an open and shut case, Aunt Jess."

"Yes, that's what the jury thought. But I still know Lee didn't kill Austin!"

"Why?"

"Because she said she didn't!"

"That's not very good evidence. I've heard that very few criminals admit they did a crime."

"Lee wouldn't lie! If she said she didn't, she didn't!"

"How did Lee account for her fingerprints on the wrench?"

"She testified that she picked up the wrench and threatened Austin with it. She said he had slapped her and was beginning to get really rough with her and that she was afraid. But she said he just hooted at her, telling her she didn't have the nerve to strike him."

"And turned his back to her to prove it?"

"I know it sounds crazy, but that is exactly what she said he did."

"That was a pretty dumb thing to do."

"That's what the jury thought, too. But Lee declares she didn't touch him with the wrench. She just dropped the wrench and ran back upstairs, leaving him below, alive and laughing at her."

"Where was the wrench found?"

"Beside the body."

"And with all that evidence against her, Lee still contends she didn't kill her husband?"

"She swore under oath that she didn't. I know it looks bad, but I still don't believe she killed Austin," Jessica said adamantly.

"Who do you think did, then?"

"I have no idea. As I said, lots of people would have been happy to see him dead. He was a despicable, cruel man. Even as a child he had a mean streak. Your mother often worried about him. If she had been well and could have raised him, he might have been a different person. But poor Ellen was bedfast so much of the time, as you well know, and there was nothing she could do but talk to him."

"Cyrus was the one who ruined him," Elliott said bitterly. "Giving him everything his heart desired and letting him treat people any way he wanted with impunity warped Austin. He gloated at the power he had over all of us and made our lives miserable. I have hated Austin Barfield almost from the time he was big enough to toddle!"

Distress flooded Jessica's face, and she laid her hand on his arm. "Elliott, the man is dead, and hate is a destructive force. It only hurts you. What possible harm can it do to Austin? Let it go. Ellen would never want you to hate your brother."

"I'll hate him as long as I live! And he was only my *half*-brother. Fortunately, Cyrus Barfield is not *my* father!"

"Ellen used to say that God could help a person get rid of hate."

"I don't want to get rid of it," Elliott said through clenched teeth. "I *want* to hate Austin. He deserves to be hated!"

"Your mother never hated anyone," Jessica said softly. "Ellen told me that God expects us to forgive others if we want Him to forgive us. She wasn't even bitter at God because she was sick for so long."

Jessica looked in Elliott's face and said softly, "I used to deeply resent my father because he never had a kind word for me. I tried to forgive him as I grew older, but I never could—until I let Jesus into my heart and found the peace Ellen had."

"Your God let my mother die!"

"Ellen did not want to leave you and Austin," Jessica said. "But there is time for each of us to die. And, Elliott, she told me that she longed to go to be with Jesus. She said she didn't understand a lot of things in the Bible but one thing she was sure of: that God loved her and that she was going to be with Him when she died...and your father."

Suddenly Jessica's eyes filled with tears and she said brokenly, "Ellen had no fear of death, Elliott. And I always lived in terror of death. I toyed with the thought of giving my life to Christ but kept putting it off...and was miserable and unhappy."

Elliott was amazed. Jessica had always seemed to be the most contented, happiest person he knew. She was successful in her chosen field and had always seemed to be so in control of her life. It was a little frightening to find that she hadn't considered herself good enough to go to heaven. She had always been the best person—outside of his mother—that he had ever known.

Clumsily he patted her hand and spoke huskily, "Aunt Jess, you were always a good woman. You shouldn't have worried. If anyone goes to heaven, you would have."

"No–no, that's not true," Jessica denied. "Ellen showed me in the Bible where I had to accept Jesus as my personal Savior. I had never done that. I–I was afraid He might want me to do something I wouldn't want to do—like be a missionary."

"You—a missionary?" Elliott laughed aloud. "That, I could

never imagine! But you have given the world knowledge about hummingbirds that...."

But Jessica was not listening to him; she continued in an agitated voice, "Many years ago when I was a child, I heard a missionary speak. I felt then that if I ever gave my heart to Jesus, He would send me to a faraway mission field. I loved Coppercrest and didn't want to leave my comfortable home."

She hesitated and then went on in a grieved voice, "How utterly foolish I was. I have traveled far from home many times, even to other countries, lived in jungles, and what have I done with my life? Just gathered some information about birds! And all of these years I could have been helping people!"

"But, Aunt Jess, being a naturalist is a worthy vocation! And you are a good one!"

"I know," Jessica sighed, "I'm not saying it isn't. But it isn't much when you were called to do something much more worthwhile. I read in Ellen's Bible one time that if we hold on to our lives, we will lose them but if we give them to God, we will have them. I hung on to mine, and it tastes like ashes in my mouth!"

"But you said you accepted Christ recently!"

Sorrowfully, Jessica laid her soft hand on his arm. "Yes, I did, but my happiness is bittersweet. It grieves me that I have so little time left to do what God called me to do years ago. Dear Elliott, I hope you don't make the mistake I did."

Jessica turned abruptly and left the room.

14

Tilda was laying lunch on a small table in Steven's room when Elliott arrived a few minutes later. As soon as Elliott entered, Steven came quickly to him with shining eyes, slipped a shy hand into Elliott's large one, and led him to a place at the table. Elliott was touched—in spite of the fact that Steven was Austin's son—that the child seemed so pleased to have him there.

Tilda had her usual smile for Elliott but pointedly ignored Allyssa until the table was set. "You can take the food off the cart and fill the plates, Allyssa," she said tartly and left abruptly.

"And how have you offended our usually smiling housekeeper?" Elliott asked with a grin.

Allyssa's chin went up and her grey-blue eyes smoldered. "Our dear housekeeper thinks her son owns me. I told her that part of your job was being with Steven as much as possible and lunching together would help you get to know each other better."

"I take it that you usually have your meals with Gentry," Elliott said. "I don't want to cause trouble between you two."

"I don't like anyone telling me what I have to do!" Her voice was tipped with acid. "Tilda said Gentry wouldn't like to hear that we were having a cozy little lunch together while he ate alone."

Steven had been taking all of this in with wide hazel eyes. Suddenly he said eagerly, "I don't mind if you go eat with Gentry, Miss Star."

Allyssa looked quickly at Steven and then said lightly, "Well, maybe I should go where I'm really wanted and eat with Gentry after all."

Was there hurt in her expressive eyes, in spite of her bantering tones? Elliott wondered. Very likely Steven's desire to send Allyssa to eat with Gentry had nothing to do with Allyssa at all. Steven obviously wanted to have his newly-arrived uncle to himself. It was a new experience that a child wanted to be with him, and in spite of himself, he was pleased.

When Elliott urged her to stay, Allyssa showed her pleasure by rewarding him with a warm smile, but Steven looked crestfallen.

Allyssa's eyes reflected the blue of her wide-skirted dress today. The simple circular neckline was adorned with a delicate silver chain from which hung a polished nugget of purest blue turquoise. For a second Elliott's eyes rested on it, then it hit him with the power of a bomb blast! He knew that nugget of turquoise! That was the stone that had hung from a heavy silver chain around Austin's neck many years ago!

"Where did you get that stone?" Elliott asked Allyssa. He tried to make his voice casual but knew it came out with a harsh edge.

"This stone?" Allyssa asked in bewilderment, lifting the nugget in one slender hand. "Did it belong to you?"

"No," Elliott said grimly, "but I know it well. It belonged to Austin Barfield when we were children." His voice roughened, "Or maybe I should say he stole it from José, our garden boy!"

Elliott's hand went to the back of his head as he said caustically, "I used to hate the sight of it hanging around Austin's neck because it reminded me of this scar he put on my neck for trying to take a hoe away from him when he attacked José because he wouldn't give him that nugget."

"How horrible!" Allyssa exclaimed. "Let me see." She moved quickly to Elliott's side and traced the deep scar with her cool fingertips.

"Your brother must have had a terrible temper," she said with a shudder. "You could have been killed!"

"Don't I know it!" Elliott said. "And I was sentenced to a week of isolation in my room because Austin told Cyrus I was at fault—and José lost his job because Austin said he stole the turquoise from our mine."

Fingering the stone, Allyssa said slowly, "I found it out in back of the house, almost buried in a flowerbed. It had an old, tarnished chain on it. I asked Tilda if it belonged to anyone in the house, and she said she was sure it didn't. So I bought a new chain for it."

"Well," Elliott said, "it's time it gave pleasure to someone."

Although he studiously avoided looking at the turquoise nugget, the lunch hour was extremely enjoyable. Allyssa was delightful company. She had a knack for making a person feel comfortable and relaxed. Encouraged by both Allyssa and Steven, Elliott soon found himself talking about his experiences in different parts of the world.

Steven was not bubbling with questions and talkative like the few children Elliott had known. Indeed, he hardly seemed like a child at all in some respects. He seldom spoke at all, but his worshipful eyes rarely left Elliott's face as he talked.

Elliott teased him and tried to draw him into the conversation as much as possible and was pleased that Allyssa did the same. Elliott found himself reluctant for the meal to end.

But after every bite of Tilda's delicious turkey pot pie and salad had been eaten and they were nibbling on homemade cookies for dessert, Allyssa suddenly looked at her watch.

"I'm about to forget! I have a dental appointment. Marvin was going to stay with Steven but he isn't back, yet. Would it be possible for you to stay with him until Marvin comes home? It shouldn't be long."

"I don't mind a bit," Elliott said. And strangely he didn't. "Cyrus seems to want me near the boy all the time, anyway. Do you have a car to drive? If not, you're welcome to mine."

"You are a jewel, but it really isn't far. The walk will do me good," Allyssa said with a warm smile.

After she had gone, Elliott—with Steven's eager help—stacked the dishes on the cart and wheeled it into the hall.

"Now, what would you like to do?" Elliott asked Steven. He felt expansive and benevolent after the meal with the attractive Allyssa and his small nephew.

"Could we go out on the deck—and maybe walk down the stairs to the street?" Steven asked hesitantly.

"Sure, why not?" Elliott was pleased that Steven wanted to go outdoors. The child looked as if he spent too little time outside.

As soon as they were at the door, Steven ran to the railing and looked down the stone stairs. "Marvin takes me down the steps sometimes," he confided. "I like climbing up and down stairs, don't you?"

"As a matter of fact, I do," Elliott said, crossing the small deck to lean on the railing. "As a kid, I climbed every stairway in town probably a hundred times a piece."

"I only get to climb on these," Steven said, "and Marvin always goes with me. He takes very good care of me," he said solemnly.

"You like Marvin real well?"

"Yeah! He plays games with me and reads to me. He even drew a picture of me!"

"He did? I'd like to see it."

"I'll get it for you," Steven said, and darted away to return almost immediately.

The drawing Steven placed proudly in Elliott's hand was drawn in pencil—and was amazingly good. There was no mistaking who the pajama-clad little boy was. Marvin had even captured the solemn expression on the child's face that he wore so often.

"Does Marvin do a lot of drawings?"

"He showed me a whole bunch one time," Steven said

eagerly. "He wants to do a kid's picture book sometime."

"Yes, I remember Marvin telling me that," Elliott said thoughtfully. "The man has real talent."

"Could we go down the stairs, now?" Steven asked.

"Sure," Elliott had hardly got the word out of his mouth when Steven—like a frisky puppy—scrambled down the stone treads into the tiny garden below.

"Hey, take it easy," Elliott said as he came leaping down to stand beside him. "Your grandfather will be very unhappy with me if you get a skinned knee or a broken arm!"

Steven looked up at Elliott with big, serious grey eyes, "Grandfather wouldn't want me to get hurt, but he doesn't really like me."

"Of course he does," Elliott aid. "He likes you so well that he had me come clear out here to help take care of you for awhile!"

But Steven shook his head stubbornly. "No, he doesn't like me. He just doesn't want my mother to take me away because then he wouldn't have anyone to run Gypsy Blue Enterprises when he can't."

Elliott was amazed at Steven's perception. It brought back vivid memories of himself as a child, longing for Cyrus to give him even a few words of kindness. But none had ever come. Would that happen to Steven also? He felt his throat tighten.

A fierce anger ripped through him. Why should Cyrus be allowed to ruin all the young lives he came in contact with? He felt a crazy compulsion to grab this small boy and flee this house forever.

"A–are you mad at me?" Steven was staring up at Elliott, dismay stamped vividly on his small, thin face.

Elliott reached out to rumple Steven's soft, pale brown hair. "I'm not mad at you, buddy! I was just thinking. Let's do some stairs-climbing!"

The concern vanished instantly from the small boy's face and a grin appeared. Steven led the way down a short sidewalk to the gate. As Elliott lifted the latch on the gate, he saw a large, heavy, power lawn mower near the fence on the neatly manicured patch of lawn. The air smelled of fresh-cut grass.

"That's an awfully big lawn mower to mow such a little lawn." He spoke his thoughts aloud to Steven, but his nephew didn't answer. He had wriggled through the partly-open gate and was already bouncing down the aged stone steps like a rubber ball. Elliott latched the gate and followed more slowly but with amusement curving his lips.

A high wall rose on either side of the stairway. It was like a long stone and concrete ladder that stretched from the back of the house to the street far below. Elliott could see a metal gate at the bottom of the canyon of stone steps.

They were halfway down when Elliott saw Steven stoop to pick up something. When Elliott leaped down the few steps to stand beside the boy, he drew in his breath sharply. Steven was holding a small, leather-bound book in his hand—Ellen Barfield's Bible!

"That's mine!" Elliott said. "Do you know how it got out here on the stairs?"

"I just found it," Steven said, pointing to the step. The child opened the book curiously. "It looks awful old," he said.

"Yes, it belonged to my mother—your grandmother," Elliott said. "Someone took it out of my room yesterday. Do you know anything about that, Steven?"

"I didn't take it," Steven quickly denied.

"No, of course you didn't, but I thought you might have seen someone else in my room or with the Bible."

But Steven's attention was no longer on what Elliott was saying. He had sat down on a step and was turning the pages. Suddenly, he held up the book for Elliott to see. "Look, there's something written in it. What does it say?"

As Elliott bent to see the words, he felt something akin to an electric shock strike him under the ribcage. In the margin of the Bible, his mother had written nine words:

"Elliott, please do not hate your father and brother."

Elliott reached out and took the Bible from Steven's hand with a slightly unsteady hand. He could almost hear his mother's soft voice speaking the words she had written in her neat, concise handwriting.

Looking closer, he saw that the words were written next to an underlined verse in First John. He read the verse aloud.

"But he that hateth his brother is in darkness, and walketh in darkness, and knoweth not whither he goeth, because that darkness hath blinded his eyes."

"You're right, Mother," Elliott mused, "I guess you did know how much I hated Cyrus and Austin. I always thought I wanted to hold on to that hate, but it's like a cancer inside of me, eating me alive. Yet, I don't know how to get rid of it."

"Who are you talking to?" Steven's puzzled words brought Elliott back to reality with a jolt. He was embarrassed.

"Let's go on down the steps," Steven said when Elliott didn't answer him immediately.

"Sure," Elliott said, slipping the Bible into his jacket pocket.

But they had aken only one step when Elliott heard a clatter at the top of the stairway far above them. Turning quickly, Elliot stared for a stunned, horror-stricken second. Careening and tumbling down the narrow rock stairway, heading straight for them, was the large, heavy lawn mower.

15

Elliott's eyes darted about for an avenue of escape and saw only one narrow chance. Snatching Steven from the steps beside him, he swung him high over his head to the top of the wall beside them.

"Hang on!" he shouted.

Then, bending his knees, he sprang for the top of the wall. As he clung there with his fingertips, desperately digging his toes into the rough wall to pull himself higher, he felt a sharp stab of pain in the calf of his right leg as the mower swept below them. Its handle struck his leg as it swept past.

He looked up to see Steven staring after the mower, grey eyes wide with fear in his white face. Elliott turned his head just in time to see the mower hit the steel gate with a thundering crash.

"That—that thing n–nearly ran over us." Steven's voice was high-pitched, like the bleat of a frightened lamb.

Elliott raked his eyes over the stairs above them. There was no one in sight. The gate was wide open, but the high, clipped hedge shut off the view into the yard. Above the little garden, on the stairs and on his own little deck, he could see no one.

Dropping to the steps, Elliott almost collapsed. His right leg buckled as the force of the drop sent a shaft of sickening pain into the calf of his leg.

He stood for a moment, leaning against the wall and resting his weight on his left leg until the pain subsided.

"Are—are you okay?" came Steven's anxious voice from above him.

Elliott breathed deeply for a moment, then said as steadily as he could, "Sure, kid, I'm okay. Just got a nasty blow on my leg. Do you think you can turn around and slide down the wall? I'll catch you."

Elliott saw the uncertainty and fear on Steven's face.

"Just turn around slowly and hang onto the top of the wall," Elliott instructed. "Then slide down and I'll catch you."

"O–okay."

"Easy, now," Elliott said as Steven turned onto his stomach, clinging to the top of the wall.

"Are—are you sure you'll catch me?"

"I'll catch you. Don't you worry about that." Elliott placed his throbbing right leg next to the wall and moved his left leg out from his body to brace himself on the stone step.

"Okay, slide down the wall," Elliott urged the reluctant child.

Steven slowly lowered his body until he was clinging by his hands to the top of the wall.

"Let go—now!" Elliott ordered.

With a frightened glance down, Steven let go. Elliott caught him and eased him to the step.

Elliott steeled himself against the pain that washed over him again in sickening waves from his injured leg and looked down at Steven who stood against him.

Steven looked up at him and laughed triumphantly, "That wasn't so bad!"

Elliott chuckled grimly. "You're not kidding. It could have been a lot worse!" He eased himself down to the step and pulled up his trouser leg to look at his leg. A dark, angry-looking lump was already swelling out on his leg. He felt it gingerly and winced.

"Does it hurt awful bad, Uncle Elliott?"

"Well, it doesn't feel so good. Let me see if I can walk." Elliott raised himself slowly to his feet and then sat back down abruptly. Perspiration flooded his forehead and trickled down under his arms. Any weight on the leg meant searing pain.

He was about to send Steven to the house for help when he heard footsteps clattering down the stairs. He looked up to see Gentry and Marvin running down the steep stairway and beyond them, he could see Tilda standing in the open gate.

"What happened?" Gentry asked as he leapt down to stand just above them.

"The big mower that was in the yard up there nearly ran us down," Elliott said. "It's down there," he motioned down the stairs where the wreckage could be clearly seen against the gate.

Marvin had stopped just behind Gentry. His dark eyes flicked anxiously from Elliott to Steven, "Are either of you hurt?"

"Uncle Elliott has a big, bad looking bump on his leg," Steven said, laying his small hand on Elliott's knee.

"Let me see," Gentry said as he knelt to examine the huge bump. "Does it feel like anything is broken?" he asked.

"No, but it hurts like mischief when I try to put any weight on it," Elliott said. "I'm going to need some help to get back to the house."

"That's no problem," Gentry said. "Marvin and I'll get you up those steps in a jiffy."

A few minutes later Elliott was stretched out on the bed in his room with his leg on a pillow. Steven hovered near the bed while Tilda disinfected the abrasion over the dark, raised bruise on his leg and applied a cold pack. She tried to get him to allow them to take him to the doctor, but Elliott refused.

She did, however, insist on giving him a cup of hot tea and some aspirin and that he readily accepted.

Marvin tried to take Steven away to his room, but he adamantly refused to go. "Uncle Elliott needs me," he declared, and Elliott grinned and told him to let the boy stay.

Elliott couldn't recall when anyone left the room. Hours later, he awoke to find the shades drawn and everyone gone. There was still a dull pain in his leg, but when he drew back the sheet, he saw that some of the swelling was already gone.

Elliott lay in the darkened room and went over the accident—if it was an accident, he told himself grimly—in his mind. Carefully, he retraced his actions before he and Steven started down the stone stairway.

He had opened the gate, and Steven had squeezed through before it was fully open. The heavy power mower had been standing back from the fence. Was there a slight slope to the yard—enough to cause the machine to slip off the grass and come tumbling down the tunnel-like steps? He couldn't remember and decided to check that out as soon as possible.

"Even if the lawn mower slid off the grass, I'm sure I pushed that gate latch back into place," Elliott muttered aloud. "And the gate should have stopped it. It couldn't have gotten enough momentum in that short a space to tear off the latch.

"Someone opened the gate and pushed that heavy mower onto the stairway!" His spoken words started a cold tremor shuddering down Elliott's spine. "Someone tried to mangle—or kill—both Steven and me!"

Could it be possible that Cyrus was right and that Steven—and now probably he as well—were in danger? But who would want Steven and him dead? Cyrus had said he no longer trusted Gentry. Was the man capable of attempted murder? It sounded too fantastic to consider. But the man had arrived on the scene very quickly!

And so was Marvin. But surely he would have no motive. He was tireless in his devotion to the small Barfield heir.

"The one thing I do know," Elliott said aloud to the empty room, "is that if I had not thought and moved as quickly as I did, both Steven and I would be in the hospital—or the morgue—right now!"

16

A sudden tap sounded at the door and in answer to his call to enter, Marvin came into the room carrying a pair of crutches.

"Mr. Barfield wants you to come to his room immediately, if you are able to get there," Marvin said. "Do you feel like trying it, sir?"

"I'll just have to see," Elliott said. He felt groggy but when he swung his feet to the floor, pain shot like fire up the calf of his leg. He sat very still for a moment, waiting for the pain to diminish, then reached for the crutches.

With Marvin balancing him, he slowly swung his body to a standing position on the crutches. When he moved his leg, the pain became a barely tolerable throb.

"Cyrus's business with me had better be important," Elliott growled. "This leg sure feels better laying in bed."

"There's a small lift down the hall, sir," Marvin said. "Perhaps you had better let me take you down in that."

With Marvin's assistance, Elliott was soon seated in an armchair in Cyrus's room. Marvin brought an ottoman for Elliott's leg and departed.

Elliott thought his stepfather's face looked more drawn and haggard today than usual.

"Did the doctor have a good report on the condition of your health today?" Elliott asked.

"About the same," Cyrus said, "but I didn't get you out of bed to talk about my health. Marvin said someone tried to kill you and Steven a while ago!"

"Well, it could have been an accident," Elliott said slowly. "I want to check and see if the weight of that lawn mower broke the latch on the gate as soon as I can get around better."

"It wasn't an accident!" Cyrus said brusquely. "Marvin checked the latch on the gate as soon as they got you back in the house. It had been tampered with; Marvin found fresh marks of a tool on it. Someone loosened the latch so it didn't catch. That *someone* wants us to think the lawn mower accidentally ran off the grass and down those steps."

Elliott felt an icy breath seem to blow across the back of his neck. Someone—maybe even someone in this household—had attempted to murder or seriously hurt Steven—and him!

"Who do you think did this?" Elliott asked.

"I wish I knew," Cyrus responded heatedly. "It could be Lee." He lowered his voice, "Or it could be someone here at Coppercrest. I don't trust anyone!"

"Should we report it to the police?"

"They'd just think this was an accident—just like they did a while back when something else like this happened to Steven!"

Elliott sat up quickly, and then grimaced as a sharp pain lanced through his leg. "You mean a similar incident happened before?"

Cyrus nodded his silvery head. "Allyssa had taken Steven shopping. They were crossing the street when a car apparently lost its brakes and came straight for him. He had run ahead of Allyssa, and the car almost hit him. It had been parked on the steep street just above the crosswalk. Steven saw it and jumped out of the way just a second before it hit him, Allyssa said. She was almost in hysterics when she got home, and Steven was so shaken up he had nightmares that night."

"Did anyone check to see who the car belonged to? Was it wrecked?"

"Yes, it piled up across the intersection against a parked car. Allyssa said the owner of the runaway car came running out of a store and swore he had put the car in gear, had the emergency brake on, and had the wheels turned into the curb. He seemed convinced someone had deliberately tampered with the car."

"But the police still thought it was an accident?"

"The chief said everyone is convinced the man wasn't at fault."

"What did Allyssa think?"

"Well, she didn't say much at the time, but after everyone else thought I was just being paranoid about Steven, she said it probably was only an accident. But I still think it was a deliberate attempt on Steven's life. Lee had escaped from prison a short while before, and we had already gotten a couple of those letters I showed you."

He paused and then said thoughtfully, "I have begun to wonder if Lee's time in prison affected her mind. Those notes don't sound very sane to me."

"Aunt Jessica doesn't think the notes are coming from Lee," Elliott said.

"Jessica wouldn't believe anything bad about Lee if she saw it happen!" Cyrus snorted. "She even stood up for her at the trial—as a character witness—and with all the evidence against the girl!"

"So you really think Lee pushed that mower off today, too?"

"Probably. But even if it wasn't Lee, Steven obviously needs someone I can trust to protect him. That's why I sent for you. But from now on, I want you to be very careful—and don't trust anyone yourself, either. I would feel better if Steven slept in your room from now on."

"I'm afraid I haven't done a very good job of taking care of Steven so far," Elliott said ruefully. "I almost let him get killed today."

"I'm satisfied with the job you did today," Cyrus said. "With anyone else he would be dead or horribly mangled right now. You protected him when there was almost no chance he could escape. It just proves I was right about your abilities when I sent for you."

In spite of himself, Elliott felt a surge of pleasure at Cyrus's words. It was the first time he could remember ever pleasing his stepfather. "Whoever did this will probably try again," Elliott said. "I wonder if I should take the child away for a while—at least until his mother is back in prison."

"No. I'm sure you can protect him here." Cyrus rejected the idea instantly. "Just be very, very careful. Steven is all I have left of Austin. He stays at Coppercrest."

When Elliott swung out of the small elevator a few minutes late, Jessica was waiting for him.

Falling in beside him, she said, "Elliott, Marvin just told me about your narrow escape on the stairs. Would you come to my suite and tell me what happened?"

Elliott's leg was throbbing and for a moment he thought of begging off, but she looked so worried, he consented. "Just let me check and see that Allyssa is still with Steven," he said.

When he knocked on Steven's room, Allyssa opened the door. Before she could say anything, Steven crowded under her arm and asked anxiously, "Is your leg okay, now, Uncle Elliott?"

"Well, it's better," Elliott said, reaching out and drawing him out the door. "Let's run up to Aunt Jess's room for a few minutes, okay?" The enormity of their near mishap fell down over him like a dark cloud, and he was suddenly hesitant to leave the boy with only the fragile Allyssa to protect him.

"It's nearly his dinnertime," Allyssa protested. "I like to have Steven on a set schedule. Children need..."

"We won't be long," Elliott interrupted.

With his eyes shining like stars, Steven eluded Allyssa's reaching hand and skipped off down the hall.

A frown briefly darkened Allyssa's face, then she shrugged and smiled, "You're the boss, Mr. Barfield said. But please don't be long. Marvin will be here any minute to stay with Steven. I'll go on down to dinner. I hope we see you there."

When they entered Jessica's apartment, Elliott saw Steven's

quick, eager eyes roving about the room.

Elliott let himself down gingerly onto a velvet couch opposite the chair Jessica had settled into. Jessica opened her mouth to speak when Steven spoke excitedly.

"Look, Uncle Elliott! Aunt Jessica has a picture a lot like mine!"

Elliott glanced at the picture Steven was pointing to, on the wall just beyond Jessica's chair. It was a charcoal drawing of Jessica.

"That is nice, Steven," Elliott agreed. "Who did the drawing of you, Aunt Jess?" he asked. "It's a very good likeness."

Jessica twisted around to look at the picture before she answered, "Oh, I've had that up so long I had almost forgotten it was there. Lee, Steven's mother, made that and gave it to me before Steven was born."

A cold chill prickled the hair on Elliott's neck and traced an icy finger down his back.

"It looks like the one Marvin made of me," Steven persisted, standing on tiptoe so he could see the drawing better. "Don't you think so, Uncle Elliott?"

"I–I didn't know Marvin drew." Jessica seemed suddenly flustered. "But–but I suppose most drawings in charcoal look much alike."

Elliott drew himself up on the crutches once more and hopped over to look at the drawing. The chill began to seep into the very marrow of his bones as he stared at the charcoal drawing. Steven was right—the style of the drawing was almost identical to Steven's.

Forcing himself to act as natural as possible even though his nerves were quaking from the magnitude of what it meant if the pictures *were* drawn by the same person, Elliott returned to his seat.

He was amazed when he heard himself speak normally, "Nice picture. Lee must be a talented girl. I didn't know she was an artist."

"Hardly an artist," Jessica said quickly. "She just dabbled a little—like a lot of people do.

Abruptly, she jumped up and took a large book from a nearby table, handing it to Steven. "You should enjoy this. It's my book on hummingbirds and has a lot of pictures."

Steven sat on the carpet and was quickly engrossed in the colorful pages.

"Now," Jessica said, returning to her chair, "tell me all about what happened this afternoon on the outside stairway."

Elliott told her all the details of what happened, but as he talked, he observed Jessica intently. Normally a placid, calm person, ever since Steven had called attention to the drawing on the wall, she had been ill-at-ease and nervous. He wasn't even sure she was listening to his account of their mishap part of the time.

Elliott's thoughts raced like a runaway truck down a steep grade. Had Jessica helped Steven's mother escape? How was the chauffeur related to Lee? Was he a spy? Another thought, even more preposterous, flitted through his mind. He shook his head. It couldn't be, but he meant to find out the truth as soon as possible. If Lee was responsible for the incident this afternoon, she was extremely dangerous!

17

All through dinner Elliott pondered the best way to find out the truth. Cyrus was having his meal in his room, and Allyssa was trying unsuccessfully to draw Elliott into the conversation—in spite of Gentry's sullen looks her way. But when Elliott only answered her questions briefly and seldom added anything more, she turned her attention to Gentry and coolly ignored Elliott the rest of the meal.

Elliott's leg hurt and he was growing increasingly apprehensive about leaving Steven alone with Marvin, so before dessert was served, he rose awkwardly on the crutches and excused himself. "My leg hurts like a toothache," he said truthfully, "so I think I'll go to my room. I'm not very good company anyway," he added with an apologetic, faint grin at Allyssa. His heart did a quick leap when she returned his smile.

Tilda entered the room at that moment with dessert and Elliott said, "Tilda, would you have John bring a small bed into my room for Steven? Cyrus thinks it best that Steven sleep in my room for awhile."

"I'll have it sent right up," Tilda said. "I think Lee Barfield is crazy as a heifer on loco weed. Imagine, trying to kill her own son—and her brother-in-law!" she fumed.

"Mother," Gentry said reprovingly, "Lee might try to frighten Cyrus, but I cannot believe she would intentionally harm Steven!"

"Well, *I* don't think it was an accident, and I'm sure Lee did it!" Tilda said stubbornly. "She went to pieces during the trial, and I think she's deranged and might do anything!"

Tilda's words prompted Elliott to change his plans. Before returning to his room, he decided to do a little snooping in Marvin's room. Quickly scanning the hall and seeing no one, he moved as quickly as he could down the hall toward the garage. He hoped Marvin was housed in the same small suite that was used by the former chauffeur. Thankfully, it was on the first floor at the back of the house, not far from the four-car garage.

When Elliott arrived at the small apartment, he looked around carefully before he tapped on the door. He didn't expect an answer since Marvin was supposed to be with Steven—but he was still relieved when no one answered his knock. He tried the knob, and it turned easily in his hand.

Easing himself inside, Elliott closed the door and switched on the light. Going quickly to the closet in the combination bedroom/sitting-room, he flipped through the clothes on the hangers. This *was* Marvin's room. Several neatly creased and cleaned chauffeur uniforms hung in the closet.

Elliott moved across the room and searched the bathroom. He had no clear idea of what he was looking for, but he hoped to find something which would either prove or disprove the impossible idea that had taken root in his mind.

A faint, but grim grin came over his face after he had finished a quick survey of the room and its contents. Nowhere in the room did he find a man's razor—or scissors—which a man would need to shave and trim a beard. But he did find a small ladies' leg-shaver.

Under the mattress, he discovered a folder of drawings, some in pencil and some in charcoal. Only one—a small charcoal of a baby—bore any artist identification. He drew in his breath sharply when he saw the initials "LB" artistically woven into a corner, in script. Lee Barfield, almost certainly.

He was about to leave when his searching hand found what felt like a small cardboard box, pushed to the back of the top shelf of a small cupboard which contained cups, instant coffee, tea, and a few other snack items.

Using his crutch, he drew the box out where he could reach it. Balancing himself on the crutches, Elliott opened the box and let out a low whistle. The box contained a small bottle of brown hair dye and a dark brown beard and mustache.

Elliott closed the box and was about to return it to the shelf when he heard a quick footstep at the door. Clumsy on the crutches, Elliott took only one step before the door swung open and Marvin stepped into the room.

Marvin's eyes went wide with shock, and then anger flamed there. "What are you doing in my room?" he demanded. Marvin's eyes went to the cardboard box in Elliott's hand. Fear flashed in his eyes, than a mask slipped over his face and Marvin asked stiffly, "What is going on? Am I suspected of a theft or something?"

"*Something* would be more like it...Lee Barfield," Elliott said grimly.

Marvin flinched as if he had been struck, but tried to regain his composure. "I don't know what you are talking about!"

"I think you do!" Elliott opened the box and took out the bottle of dye. "Brown hair dye, a beard and mustache!"

"So! Lots of people change the color of their hair. And if I choose to wear a beard—even a false one—what does it matter as long as I do my work well?"

"Why don't we sit down and talk?" Elliott said slowly.

Elliott plunked down heavily in a straight chair and Marvin backed away and sat down, wary and stiff, on the bed. The chauffeur lifted a hand to push back his hair and Elliott saw that it was trembling almost uncontrollably.

"I found the drawings—under your mattress," Elliott said patiently, his eyes boring into Marvin's. When the chauffeur only stared at him, Elliott continued, "Steven showed me the drawing you did of him. By the way, you are very good."

Marvin's eyes made Elliott think of a rabbit's eyes, petrified as it stares into the eyes of a rattlesnake.

"Aunt Jessica has a drawing that Lee Barfield drew of her several years ago. Even Steven immediately knew the same person had drawn his and Jessica's likenesses."

Suddenly Marvin seemed to crumple. He dropped his eyes and clasped his long slim fingers tightly together. "What–what are you going to do?" The words—so low he could scarcely hear them—seemed wrung from the now trembling, ashen lips.

"That depends on what you have to tell me," Elliott said gravely. He steeled himself against pity. Lee might be a murderer—of her husband, and also an attempted murderer of himself—and of her own son.

"Who is with Steven?" Elliott asked, suddenly remembering that Marvin was supposed to be with the boy.

Straightening his shoulders and sucking in a ragged breath of air, Marvin lifted dark, misery-filled eyes to Elliott. "John is with him. He came to set up a portable bed for Steven in your room. Steven had asked at dinner if we could play a new game I bought recently, so I asked John to stay with Steven while I came to my room to get the game."

"Good, he'll be all right for now. Now, Marvin—or I should say Lee?" Elliott smiled faintly. "It's hard to call you that. You certainly do not look like the Lee in your pictures and Gentry's videos."

Marvin said nothing so Elliott said pointedly, "You were much heavier then; you had light brown hair, copper-flecked gold eyes and a soft, husky voice. In fact you were a very feminine woman. And now..."

Lee's head came up. "Prison will change a lot of things." Lee's voice was bitter and her eyes cold and hard as she interrupted. "You are right! I used to look soft. I was soft! Anyone could push me around. Especially my handsome husband!"

Scorching fire smoldered in her eyes. "Austin knocked me around and only sneered when I cried and pled with him not to hurt me! And when I finally worked up enough courage to leave him, he came after me and told me that if I ever left him again, he would take Steven away from me, and I would never see him again!"

Her voice broke and she had to swallow hard before rushing on. "So I knuckled under and took his abuse—even when he broke my arm once!"

"Why didn't you tell someone?"

"I tried to tell his father!" Her voice shook with emotion. "But he just became very angry and told me to never tell him such lies again!"

"Why didn't you go to the police?"

Lee gave him a withering look. "Mr. Barfield told Austin what I had said. Austin was so furious that he beat me worse than he ever had. He threw me against a wall and that's when he broke my arm. I hit my head on something and blacked out—or he would probably have killed me.

"When I came to, he told me that if I ever again told anyone that he abused me, he *would* kill me. Even if he had to track me to the ends of the earth!"

"You killed Austin, then?"

"No, I didn't have the nerve! We had had an argument that afternoon, and I picked up a heavy pipe wrench and told him I was going to hit him if he tried to hurt me again. He had already slapped me a couple of times."

"What was the argument about?"

Lee clenched her hands together until the knuckles shone white and tormented. "I suspected Austin was seeing another woman. I accused him and he denied it and slapped me. Then I told him that we needed some time apart and that he should get some counseling about his violent temper and his abusive behavior."

"It would have taken some powerful counseling to break Austin from hurting people," Elliott said acidly. "I know. I was one of his victims—and so was nearly everyone who knew him!"

"He was so sweet before we were married, I never suspected he was that way," Lee said. She paused and then said softly, "But you know, as crazy as it sounds, I still loved Austin. In spite of the many times he hit me and raged and swore at me.

"I wanted to go away for awhile and take Steven—who was just a baby then. I really hoped if we were away from each other for a few months, and he got treatment for his violent behavior, that we could still build a good marriage." Her voice trembled. "I loved him so."

"And you told him you wanted him to get treatment?"

"Yes, and he just laughed at me! He said there was nothing wrong with him. That *I* was to blame for everything. He said I drove him to violence with my nagging."

Lee locked eyes with Elliott. "Do you know that I really believed I was to blame when he beat me? Over and over, I tried to do everything just right so it wouldn't bring out the violence in him. But it never worked."

"What happened when you threatened to strike Austin with the pipe wrench?"

"He just stood there and laughed at me—scornfully. I think he was hoping I *would* try to hit him, so he would have an excuse to beat me up again. But I threw the wrench down and ran upstairs and locked my doors."

"What happened then?"

"As I ran up the stairs, I was thinking that I had to get away from him before he killed me—or maybe even our baby. He had never struck Steven, but the day before he had yanked him out of bed and shook him violently when he wouldn't stop crying."

"But you didn't leave?"

"I didn't get the chance. Crying like a big baby, I was packing a suitcase when I heard shouts down in the garden where I had left Austin. Then I heard Tilda scream. I unlocked the door and ran out on the deck. Austin was lying on the ground, and I could see blood on the grass.

"I rushed down the stairs and gathered Austin's head up in

my arms. Blood was gushing from a wound on the back of his head.

"His father was standing there and he looked at me with the blackest hatred possible in his eyes. 'You killed my son!' he shouted. For a minute, I thought he was going to attack me. Horrified that anyone would think I had killed Austin, I began to stammer out a denial but he cut me off.

"'I heard you arguing with Austin!' Mr. Barfield just spit out the words. 'I heard you threaten Austin. You killed my son!' He began to cry then, horrible cries of agony and grief. And if Gentry had not held him, I think he would have tried to tear me apart. I was terrified.

"Then the police came and took me away. I was glad that my son was only a baby and wasn't old enough to know his father had been murdered and that he didn't see his mother taken to prison. He slept through it all."

"Tilda said you went to pieces at the trial."

Suddenly Lee straightened and steel seemed to firm her voice. "Yes, it was the most horrible experience of my life. In spite of all he had done to me, I still loved Austin. On top of my agonizing grief for the loss of my husband was the nightmare of the weeks in jail and then the trial. When I was actually convicted of killing Austin, I thought I would go mad. It was so unfair!

"And I had no one to stand with me—except Jessica, bless her heart! She was away when Austin died, but she came home as soon as she heard. Not that she could do much for me at the trial but she did what she could—and she visited me in jail." Lee's voice broke for a moment, "I will never forget what she did for me!"

"Jessica helped you to escape, didn't she?"

Lee looked up quickly and said with finality, "No! I'm sure she wasn't the one who planned and aided my escape, but I'm still puzzled about who did. Someone paid a guard to give me an opportunity to escape. I didn't understand why someone would do this for me, or who it was, but I grabbed the chance."

"Perhaps Jessica got you out but didn't want you to know."

"No, when I got out I was instructed to go to a certain place and wait for someone to come and take me away. But I was afraid to do that since I had no idea who was in back of my escape.

"So, as soon as I was free I put on this disguise. I had planned ever since I was imprisoned what I would do if I ever escaped.

"Then, I contacted Jessica. At first she was a little reluctant to help me, but when she saw how desperate I was, she plotted with a friend who was about to go abroad for the summer to give me a recommendation as a chauffeur."

"How did you learn about cars and how to care for them?"

"I took mechanic classes while I was in prison and learned everything I could about automobiles so I could make a living when, if ever, I escaped. I knew I wouldn't be able to touch my own money." She smiled triumphantly. "I can take a car apart and put it back together with the best, if I do say so. And I like it!"

"And losing weight was also part of your planned disguise?"

"Yes, I had been overweight all my life, but I determined to take that flab off or die in the effort. So I dieted and exercised until I was slim and very strong. I felt like a new person!"

"From looking at your pictures, and hearing your own testimony, I would never have thought you could discipline yourself to do all of that," Elliott said in admiration.

A slight flush of pleasure rose in Lee's face. "It wasn't easy—in fact I had a battle royal with myself nearly every moment!" Lee lifted her hands and held them out. Her fingers were long and slim but also tanned, strong and tough-looking. Definitely not the soft hands of a pampered girl.

"When I was taken back to my cell after I had been found guilty, I was crying and nearly had to be carried. I cried all night. But the next morning when I saw my soft, plump face and puffy, red eyes in the mirror, and looked at my baby-soft hands, I suddenly decided I had had enough of being soft."

"And you determined to change?"

"Yes! All my life I had pampered my flesh—and tried to please other people. It had gotten me nowhere. Unless I escaped, I would spend the rest of my life in prison with tough, hardened criminals. I knew if I didn't get tough and stay that way, things were going to be rough for me."

"How *did* you fare in prison?"

"It was brutal at first! I was beaten up a couple of times, but I took some lessons in karate from another prisoner, dieted and exercised and soon toughened up. I tried to be a friend to the other prisoners, and I practiced being fair. Soon I had friends who helped me if some of the other women got rough. I survived."

"Why did you come back here?" Elliott asked. "It looks like that was the most dangerous thing you could have done."

"I wanted to try to clear myself, if possible—and to be near my son. Coppercrest was the only place I could do both." She grinned. "And who would expect Lee Barfield, escaped convict, to return to her old home? I had practiced changing my voice all the time I was in prison so it is more natural now than my own voice."

Suddenly Lee got up and moved to stand before Elliott. Her deep blue eyes and voice were desperate. "You must believe me! I did not kill my husband!"

She laid strong, tanned, beseeching fingers on Elliott's arm. "I gave you back the paper that Austin stole from your mother, so now you are a quarter-owner of Gypsy Blue Enterprises. I helped you! Isn't it fair for you to help me? Please! I am desperate!"

Elliott felt trapped. "I have never done anything outside of the law," he said slowly. "If I don't expose you, I am guilty of breaking the law. I could go to prison for aiding and abetting an escaped criminal."

"But I'm not guilty! Someone in this house framed me. They

heard me arguing with Austin and took advantage of the situation and carried out the threat I made with the pipe wrench!"

When Elliott still looked doubtful, Lee tightened her grip on his arm convulsively. "Please! Don't you see that if we don't find out who the person is who killed Austin, he may murder Steven—and you, too!"

"Think about this," she rushed on. "What if the person who helped me escape wanted me out of prison so I could be charged with yet another crime? The murder of my son! I couldn't kill again if I was in prison. So they helped me escape.

"They could murder my son and then blame it on me! You know, the deranged mother kills her own son—as she did her husband! The crazed psychopath who couldn't bear for anyone else to have him so she murdered her own child!"

A tremor shuddered through Elliott's body and he said grimly, "You could be right."

"You believe me, then?"

"I'm too confused to really know what I believe at this point," Elliott said candidly. "But as preposterous as it all sounds, it still makes some sense."

"You won't give me away?"

Elliott hesitated a long time, looking deep into Lee's eyes. "Not yet anyway," he finally agreed reluctantly. "Have you found any evidence to back up your claims or help clear you?"

"No, not really," Lee admitted. "But I'm keeping my eyes open. Did Cyrus tell you that someone loosened the latch on the gate to make it look like the power mower slipped through the gate accidentally?"

"Yes, but Cyrus seemed to think you—or Lee, I should say—might have pushed that mower off on us."

"Well, I didn't! I'm as sane as anyone—and I would never harm my son!" Lee's dark eyes met Elliott's squarely.

Suddenly Elliott grinned. "I suppose your dark blue eyes are only colored contact lenses."

Lee showed white, even teeth in a conspiratorial grin. "Yes, I have almost perfect vision, but it was easy to get contacts. I saved the cash I had when I was arrested and bought these while I was in prison. The prison would buy us glasses but not contacts, so I paid the difference. The optometrist didn't bat an eye when I ordered dark blue lenses. I guess lots of girls order colored contacts these days."

Suddenly there was a tap on the door and Jessica's voice called, "Marvin, may I come in?"

When Jessica stepped in and saw Elliott there, she darted a quick, fearful, questioning glance at Lee.

"There's no need for secrecy now, Aunt Jess," Elliott said. "I know that Marvin is Lee."

18

Jessica turned to Elliott. "Allyssa said you were going to your room." Her voice held a slightly condemning note.

"I felt a strong compulsion to find out more about our chauffeur so I decided to detour by his room and see what I could find out—while he was supposed to be with Steven," Elliott explained.

"And he found my hair dye and my extra beard," Lee finished. She sighed. "I told him everything—and he is going to keep our secret for now."

"Good!" Jessica said to Elliott. "I was afraid you suspected something when Steven called attention to the picture Lee had drawn of me."

"That sort of cinched it, but I had already begun to wonder about Marvin," Elliott said. "Both Lee and he raise a left eyebrow when they smile—in a rather unique way."

"I didn't know that!" Lee exclaimed. "And I thought I had covered every base in my camouflage!"

"I had never noticed it either," Jessica said, and added worriedly, "I hope no one else has."

Elliott looked at Jessica. "I thought you had become a Christian. And yet you lied to me—about Lee!"

Jessica wilted before his condemning eyes. "I–I know. Ever since I started this deception, I have struggled with my conscience. I–I hope you will forgive me—and that God will. I'm sorry I deceived you. I don't know how to get out of it now without sending Lee back to prison."

"Jessica was only trying to protect me," Lee said sharply. When Elliott's steely eyes swung in her direction, she dropped her eyes. "I did much worse than Jessica. I accepted Christ as my Savior a short while before I escaped prison—and I still went ahead with my plans to escape and–and to deceive everyone at Coppercrest."

"Mother was always scrupulously honest," Elliott said bitingly. "Is this a new set of Christian standards?"

"Your mother wasn't sent to prison for something she didn't do!" Lee shot back, her deep blue eyes flashing fire.

"She would never have lied!" Elliott said angrily.

Jessica laid a gentle hand on Elliott's arm and shook it to get his attention. "You are right, Elliott. But let's not argue, please."

Lee's voice was humble as she apologized. "I'm sorry for that barb about your mother. I know that lying is wrong—but I didn't know what to do when presented with an opportunity to escape—so I–I took it and became Marvin. Please don't expose me yet. I've *got* to find out who killed Austin."

"Very well," Elliott said hesitantly. "I suppose I'm a poor one to judge either of you. Why should I judge you for standards I don't want to accept?"

"Were you looking for me?" Lee turned to ask Jessica.

"Yes, I wanted to warn you that I was afraid Elliott might be getting suspicious," Jessica said, "but it's too late for that now.

"But as I was on my way here, I had a rather troubling thought. Don't you both think it's strange that John's tools were responsible for both Austin's death and the near calamity with the lawn mower this afternoon?"

Both Elliott and Lee looked startled.

"But what motive could John possibly have for killing his employer's son?" Elliott asked, aghast.

Before Jessica could answer, Lee jumped up. "Anyone who knew Austin any length of time probably suffered at his hands at some time. And the person who murdered Austin might want to harm his son, just because he is his son! I left Steven with John and I don't want to take any chances!" Without another word, she dashed from the room.

When Elliott swung into Steven's room a few minutes later, tall, lanky John was just getting up from a chair in front of the television. Lee was across the room, laying out Steven's pajamas, as calm as if she had just strolled back to Steven's room, instead of running.

Elliott stopped just inside the door and leaned against the wall. Lee was a superb actress, there was no question about that. And a new thought struck him. For weeks Lee had so convincingly played the part of Marvin that a whole household of people, who had lived in the same house with her for years when Austin was alive, had accepted her as Marvin, the chauffeur.

Lee had to be intelligent and extremely bold to plan and carry out such a preposterous deception. Was Lee's convincing story of her innocence in Austin's murder also a clever act?

Black thoughts, like evil imps of darkness, rushed through his mind. Had Lee killed her husband after all? What if Lee had returned to kidnap her son, as the notes implied? Perhaps even to murder the child if she were thwarted in her efforts to steal him.

But hadn't there been every opportunity already to take the child away, if she had wanted to do that? Another chilling possibility presented itself: What if she were really after revenge—on Cyrus who had sent her to prison? The notes had already had a devastating affect on the sick old despot. Enough to cause him to send for Elliott!

The notes! Why had he not thought of them before? He would ask the police to have an expert compare the note he had received from Lee with the notes that had been sent before. Lee had declared that all the notes except the one she had sent to Elliott—about his document she had mailed to him at the post office—were not sent by her.

Vaguely, Elliott was aware that John had gone silently away.

Then he felt Steven tugging at his hand, trying to get his attention.

"What—what did you say?" Elliott asked.

"I asked if you wanted to play a game with Marvin and me."

Elliott didn't really feel up to playing games, but suddenly he did not want to leave the boy alone with Lee—or anyone else in this house right now.

"How about if I read you a story instead and then I think you and I had both better hit the hay, buddy," Elliott said. "We've had a little too much excitement for one day!"

"Your uncle is right," Lee readily agreed as she excused herself. "I'll see you tomorrow."

Elliott slept soundly and when he climbed out of bed the next morning, he was delighted to find that the swelling was almost gone from his leg. It was still fiery-colored, bruised, and painful, but he could walk on it without crutches.

Elliott and Steven were breakfasting in Steven's room when Allyssa came with a message from Cyrus. "Mr. Barfield wants to see you while I give Steven his morning lessons."

A heady rush of pleasure rippled through Elliott when she tilted her shapely head to look up at him with a warm smile.

"Would you like to attend a concert tonight? Gentry was supposed to take me, but Mr. Barfield is sending him out of town this afternoon on some business."

The warm glow of pleasure seemed to expand, sending tingling, pulsing warmth and joy into every vein of his body. "Sure!" He hoped his reply didn't sound as eager as he felt. "However," he added reluctantly, "we would have to take Steven along."

"Oh, I'm sure Marvin will stay with Steven. He never seems to mind."

"I wish I could do that," Elliott said truthfully. "There's nothing I'd like better than an evening out with the loveliest lady I know, but Cyrus wants me to stay close to Steven right now."

And I don't want to leave him alone that long with Lee, either, he added silently to himself.

A flash of annoyance creased Allyssa's satiny forehead. "But he is as safe with Marvin as he is with me, or you, or anyone! And besides, what could happen to him in his own room?"

For a moment Elliott almost gave in to the thought of spending an evening alone with Allyssa. He had never met anyone who made his heart do the strange things it did when he was around this lovely woman.

Then his sense of duty took over and he shook his head regretfully. "I have an obligation to Steven until things get more settled around here. I'm dreadfully sorry!"

For a moment Allyssa gazed at him with perplexed eyes, then she laughed lightly, "Of course you are right! And I like a man who takes his responsibilities seriously. We'll just take Steven along. It will be good for his education to attend a concert, anyway."

Elliott smiled and went to his room. Before he went down to see his stepfather, Elliott called and talked to the police chief. He told him about receiving the note from Lee and suggested comparing it with the writing on the other notes she was supposed to have written.

The chief thought it was an excellent idea. He said they had retained copies of the other notes.

Elliott sealed the note in an envelope and sent it over to the police station by John when he went downstairs. Then he went to Cyrus.

The old man was lying back in a reclining chair, with pillows propped about him, when Elliott entered his sitting room. His hawk-like eyes held a distinct excitement in their icy depths, Elliott's nerves tensed. What did Cyrus have up his sleeve this morning?

He wasn't long in finding out.

"Well, I see you are getting around much better today,"

Cyrus greeted him heartily, and Elliott felt a twinge of apprehension slide down his neck.

"Since you are a partner in Gypsy Blue Enterprises, I want you to begin to get acquainted with its operations and how it's run," Cyrus went on.

"Wait a minute," Elliott protested. "I'm not in the least interested in how Gypsy Blue is run. I don't plan to have any part in its operations!"

"Gentry will take you on a tour of the jewelry store and the workrooms." His stepfather continued as if Elliott had not spoken. "Later you will want to see the mine. We do business worldwide. You will be amazed at how large our operation is now."

"But—but..."

Cyrus raised his voice and called for Gentry. "I have instructed Gentry to take you on a tour and explain anything you wish to know."

Gentry must have been waiting by the door, because he entered the room almost instantly and made no attempt to hide his displeasure. His wide lips were pressed into a grim line, and his eyes glinted with green fire when they rested briefly on Elliott.

Why is he so upset? Elliott wondered uneasily, as he followed Gentry's broad back from the room and down to the elevator.

As soon as the elevator door closed on them, Gentry turned to Elliott and said savagely, "What do you mean by asking my girl for a date!"

Elliott took a quick backward step and felt the side of the elevator against his back. Gentry's big hands were white-clenched fists at his side, and his face was murderous. He hadn't realized how big Gentry was until he was caged with him in the small elevator. Powerful muscles rippled in the wide shoulders and arms, and his stocky body and thick neck reminded Elliott of a very large pit bull.

"Say, take it easy," Elliott said, lifting a placating hand. "In the first place, Allyssa said you two were not engaged or anything. And in the second place *she* asked me to take her to the concert because you were going to be out of town."

The elevator came to a halt and the door slid open, but Gentry glared at Elliott. Finally he growled in a controlled but menacing voice, his lips curling with disdain, "Who do you think you are? Coming back to Coppercrest after all these years and moving in like you owned the place!"

Elliott felt hot blood begin to pound in his veins but he fought to keep his voice calm. He had never run from a fight—and he had fought his share—but he had long ago learned that avoiding a fight was wiser, especially with an enraged man like the one who faced him.

"Gentry, I only came here because Cyrus sent for me. I will only be here for four weeks. Then I have another assignment."

Some of the tension seemed to ease out of Gentry, but he still stood like a pit bull dog. His voice was derisive. "But I'm sure you're not going to refuse whatever is offered you! You'd be a fool if you did!

"And let me tell you one thing, Elliott Fleet. I've worked hard for my position in this company; I don't plan to hand it over to Cyrus Barfield's stepson. And let my girl alone, too!"

Elliott stepped out of the elevator into a wide hall. If he had to defend himself, he wanted more space for it.

Gentry took two long steps and blocked Elliott's path. Elliott took a deep breath. His square jaw went rock hard and slightly jutting. A fire smoldered in his dark eyes and he straightened to his full six feet, two inches. He wasn't built as powerfully as Gentry, but he was an inch or so taller. His voice was quiet, deceptively so.

"It was my understanding that Allyssa was free to date whomever she liked. Until she tells me differently, I will date her anytime she accepts my invitations."

Gentry's voice was bitter. "You *are* just like your brother Austin, aren't you? If it belongs to someone else, take it—

whether you want it or not!"

Elliott stared at Gentry for a moment. What was Gentry hinting at? He said slowly, "What do you mean? What did Austin try to take away from you?"

"Anything I happened to like when I was a kid growing up with him!" Gentry said hotly. "But the last thing he tried to take away was my job—just like you obviously will try to do!"

Elliott forgot to be angry at the last remark as the implication of the first statement struck him forcefully. "Before he died Austin threatened to take away your job? Why?"

"Certainly not because I wasn't doing it well!" Gentry said bitterly. "I did all the work of running this place, both mine *and* the work Austin was supposed to do!"

"You did the work and Austin got the credit. And when Austin threatened to fire you, that was the straw that broke the camel's back—so you killed him?"

"No! I didn't kill Austin! Not because I hadn't wanted to—hadn't dreamed of doing it! But I didn't kill him. Lee did, remember?" His voice dripped sarcasm. "She was convicted in court!"

"But there seems to be a doubt in some folks' minds that she did."

Gentry's eyes flashed angrily. "You've been talking to Jessica. That old meddler wasn't even here! What does she know?"

"She said she knows Lee, and that Lee was not capable of murdering anyone, even someone who was abusing her."

"Anyone can be pushed—even a scared rabbit like Lee. And it was common knowledge in this household that Austin was beating up his wife."

"Why didn't someone do something? Report it to the police!"

"And look like a fool? And lose my job, most certainly?"

"Obviously the Deadly Blue has you enmeshed in her trap, too," Elliott muttered.

But Gentry rushed on with his defense. "The Barfields are some of the most influential people in Arizona. Austin would have denied he beat his wife—and even Lee would probably have denied it. So why get involved with an impossible situation?"

A door in the hall opened. A woman stuck her head out and addressed Gentry. "Mr. Howard, I called upstairs and your mother said you were on your way down here. There is a call for you in your office. I think it's important."

Gentry seemed to change before Elliott's eyes. The bitter, blustering man drew a deep breath and a mask fell over his face. Only a beading of moisture at his receding hairline and upper lip remained to show his former agitation. Calm, dignified, and authoritative, a man to be obeyed and looked up to, Gentry was now every inch the second-in-command at Gypsy Blue Enterprises.

"Tell whoever it is that I'll be right there," he instructed the girl. Turning to Elliott, he spoke briskly, "The workshops are down the hall and to the left. I'll meet you there as soon as I get off the phone."

Elliott was left standing in the hall with several new thoughts swirling in his head. So Austin had threatened Gentry's most prized possession—his job at Gypsy Blue Enterprises. The suave, authoritative facade Gentry used had cracked to reveal deep, violent passions. Had Gentry murdered Austin?

19

Cyrus had declared Elliott would be amazed at the size of Gypsy Blue Enterprises...and he was. There were bright, airy workshops where a number of silversmiths and other workers—mostly Navajo and Hopi Indians—created their painstaking masterpieces.

Gentry, cool, now, and impersonal, introduced Elliot to the silversmiths as Mr. Barfield's stepson and part owner of Gypsy Blue Enterprises.

Gentry led him to a table where a heavy-set, middle-aged Navajo woman was absorbed in her work. Elliott whistled softly when he saw the beauty and originality of the turquoise and silver necklace she was creating.

"Is the turquoise from Gypsy Blue Mine?" Elliott asked.

"Sure is! The Gypsy Blue Mine produces some of the most beautiful virgin turquoise in the world."

"But it isn't all blue," Elliott protested. "Part of it is green so why call it Gypsy Blue when some of it is green?"

Gentry chuckled. "Blue or green, all turquoise from the Gypsy Blue Mine is called by the Gypsy Blue trade name. In the late 1920s, when Cyrus's father bought the claim and began mining copper, he was filled with admiration for the beautiful blue turquoise in his mine."

"I recall Cyrus saying his father declared the turquoise was as pretty as a gypsy so he named his copper mine Gypsy Blue," Elliott said.

"Yet the old man never saw the possibilities in turquoise,"

Gentry said, "only metal ore. The bulk of his wealth came from copper but he also mined silver, gold, lead, zinc and manganese. He invested some of his money—when the copper began to run out—in four trading posts in Arizona and New Mexico and finally only worked the mine enough to hold the claim.

"But after the old man died, Cyrus began mining the by-products of copper: gem-quality turquoise, azurite, malachite, and chrysolite from Gypsy Blue Mine. All of it bears the Gypsy Blue trade name and is used exclusively in our jewelry.

"What about when it is all gone?"

"We'll cross that bridge when we get to it. Many of the mines in the area are depleted already, but Gypsy Blue still has plenty for our use. We have never sold our natural minerals—just used them for our own jewelry. Also, Cyrus salvaged quite a bit from his father's old mine dumps and stopes—rooms, to you.

"I had better show you the jewelry store now," Gentry said, looking at his watch. "Cyrus is sending me on a selling trip this afternoon. I'll be back tomorrow."

Carpeted in bright turquoise blue, the large jewelry store glittered and glowed with the blue and green of turquoise, the darker blue of azurite, the green of malachite, and the gold of chrysolite set in beds of silver and gold. The spectacular copper ceiling was complemented by the red brick and oak-paneled walls.

Elliott was impressed in spite of his determination not to be. He left about an hour later, amazed at the work done and the respect in which Gentry was held by everyone.

That evening, just before dinner, Cyrus called Elliott into his sitting room. He had instructed Allyssa to dress Steven to dine with the family this evening. Steven had pleaded with Elliott to beg off for him. Although sympathetic, Elliott knew there was nothing he could do. A summons from the master of Coppercrest was law.

When Elliott arrived in his stepfather's suite, Cyrus was dressed in an expensive grey suit with a burgundy tie. Although he still looked tired and old, Cyrus once again carried himself ramrod straight and commanding.

"Sit down," Cyrus commanded brusquely. When Elliott complied, Cyrus looked him full in the face.

Elliott refused to allow his eyes to drop from his stepfather's, but the muscles in his stomach bunched and twisted painfully, and he realized that his palms were wet. Why did his stepfather still have this effect on him?

"Have you decided to become Steven's guardian?"

Cyrus's voice seemed to break the spell that held Elliott. He looked away and said as firmly as his quivering nerves would allow, "I'm not sure, yet. I need a little more time." He was angry with himself that Cyrus—who was old and sick and held no tangible strings on him—could still make him feel insignificant, uneasy and as tense as a stalked animal.

Cyrus lifted an impatient, bony hand. "We may not have time for your dallying." His gimlet eyes bored into Elliott's. "Weren't you pleased with what you saw today of Gypsy Blue Enterprises?"

"You have done well with your business," Elliott agreed.

"We have connections all over the world," Cyrus bragged. "What you saw is just this end of our business. But it must have a firm, steadying hand until Steven has grown up and can take over the helm of Gypsy Blue." He leaned over and tapped Elliott's knee with a bony finger.

"But before Steven can ever take over the business, he must grow up under the guidance of a level-headed man. And you are the only one I know who can do the job and do it well."

Elliott hated himself for the burst of pride his stepfather's words gave him. What did he care what Cyrus thought of him, good or bad? But the unbelievable and incomprehensible truth was that he did care! He cared greatly.

Elliott's mind was reeling under the impact of this incredible fact, and he didn't answer Cyrus immediately.

Suddenly, his stepfather slumped back wearily into his chair and closed his eyes for a moment.

Elliott noticed the parchment thinness of his eyelids, the dark smudges beneath the sunken sockets, and the unhealthy pallor of his thin cheeks. Then a startling thought exploded in Elliott's mind.

Cyrus is dying and he knows it! That is why he is so desperate...so insistent. The thought left him strangely troubled and depressed.

Elliott realized that Cyrus had opened his eyes and was staring. When he spoke, the words were so faint that Elliott had to strain to hear them. "Don't you know what I am offering you? You will be the top man in Gypsy Blue Enterprises after I am gone. People will look up to you, and you can have your heart's desire in the way of any pleasure and comfort."

"For what is a man profited, if he shall gain the whole world, and lose his own soul? or what shall a man give in exchange for his soul?"

Elliott heard the words, and it was a shocked moment before he realized that they had come from his own mouth. A cold sweat broke out on his forehead, and his heart began to pound like waves hurling themselves upon a rocky coastline. Those words from the Bible, like distant ghosts, had risen from somewhere deep inside his memory. Had his mother planted them there many years ago, leaving them deeply buried in his subconscious mind?

Cyrus was staring at him with something akin to fear in his eyes. His voice was hoarse as he stammered, "That's—what—Ellen—always—told—me."

Abruptly he straightened, and Elliott saw him make a valiant effort to regain his composure. But his voice was still not much more than a ragged shred when he spoke again. "Nonsense! That's all it is! I'll—I'll not have you quoting Scripture to me! I–I had enough of that when Ellen was alive."

Elliott was still extremely shaken or he would not have spoken as he did to Cyrus. His tones were husky with emotion, as he said, "I didn't mean to speak those words. Indeed, I didn't even know I still knew any Bible verses. But I can almost hear Mother quoting it to me."

Cyrus's already sallow face paled even further. He took several deep breaths as if it were a struggle to get oxygen into his tortured lungs. Then he said hurriedly, "Perhaps we should go in to dinner. I expect it is ready."

"Wait," Elliott said suddenly. "I have made up my mind about Steven. If you still want me to be his guardian, I will do it!"

A relieved, satisfied smile flitted over Cyrus's face. "Good! Very good! I'll get my lawyer over here first thing in the morning. It's Saturday, but he always comes at my convenience."

He stood to his feet and took a couple of steps toward Elliott, who had also risen, and clapped his hand on his shoulder jovially. "You won't be sorry!"

A sudden despondency settled over Elliott as he followed Cyrus from the room. Was he selling his independence to his stepfather? he thought morosely. Was he, who gloried in his freedom to roam the world in search of news, tying himself to a small child? Was he also to become a captive of the Deadly Gypsy Blue?

He stifled a sudden, brief, claustrophobic panic as he entered the dining room. Perhaps he should run while he still could! But he found himself going to the table, pulling out Allyssa's chair, and seating himself between Steven and Allyssa as if his life were not being rocked by tides that might sweep away his freedom forever!

20

Sunday morning found Elliott, Marvin, Steven, and Jessica in church. As Elliott shared a songbook with his small nephew, he thought about the events of the past two days.

He had immensely enjoyed the concert with Allyssa on Friday evening. Steven had gone to sleep before the program was half over. But Elliott had relished the pleasure of sharing good music with a person of like tastes, especially one as pleasant to look at as Allyssa.

On Saturday, Allyssa had suggested a picnic in the hills. Elliott asked Tilda to prepare a lunch, but when she found out Allyssa was going with Elliott and Steven, she wouldn't even smile at Elliott and Steven when they came to get the picnic basket. And when Allyssa appeared, she had turned her back on her and refused to even speak to her.

I never remember Tilda acting this way before, Elliott pondered now. *Obviously, she feels I am stealing her son's girl...and that Allyssa is a two-timer. Well, maybe I am stealing his girl. But if Allyssa doesn't feel the same way about Gentry, then how could I be stealing what Gentry didn't have to begin with?*

Certainly it should be Allyssa's choice whom she dated. And, after all, it was Allyssa who was initiating the dates—if they could be called that—with Steven along. But Elliott wasn't entirely comfortable about the situation.

When they had returned from the hills, pleasantly tired, Cyrus had been waiting impatiently in the foyer for Elliott.

"I've decided Steven should attend church," he had declared to an astonished Elliott. "Ellen would have wished him to go. Besides, if I had insisted on Austin attending church, as his mother desired...perhaps he would still be alive today."

At Elliott's incredulity, he said defensively, "Austin was never well-liked by anyone for long. He–he made many enemies. Perhaps church would have helped him to be a more likable person."

When Elliott continued to stare in astonishment, Cyrus had dropped his eyes and finished, "I–I know I made...a few... mistakes with Austin. Mistakes I don't want us to make in rearing his son."

"So you are taking Steven to church?" Elliott asked, struggling to overcome his shock. He remembered vividly how Cyrus had always ridiculed his mother when she attended church.

"No, *you* are going to take him," Cyrus said. "I'm not quite up to going out."

"Me? I *never* go to church!" Elliott objected.

"Well, then, it is time you went, too," Cyrus said as if the matter was settled. "Now, I must get to my room." He hesitated and then spoke rapidly without looking up, "The little church your mother attended is still in town. You might want to go there. Jessica could show you where it is; she goes there some, I understand." He had shuffled away as swiftly as he could.

So here they were in his mother's church! Elliott had never been more uncomfortable in his life. A dozen times he had almost sent Steven with Martin and Jessica and stayed home.

But ever since the power mower incident, he had felt that a sword quivered over both his and Steven's heads but, especially, he feared for Steven. Even to avoid an unpleasant experience such as church, he could not entrust Steven to others. Steven was his responsibility.

If *only* he knew who had killed Austin, and who was responsible for the near mishap with the mower! But it could be anyone here—or even someone outside of Coppercrest. With his cocky arrogance and cruel nature, Austin's enemies might well include half the people in Bisbee!

The police report on the notes should tell him something. If Lee didn't write any of the notes except the one to Elliott, that would at least make her credible in his eyes.

Elliott had been surprised when Marvin—he still thought of Lee that way because the chauffeur just didn't look like a woman—asked to accompany them. Jessica had told him then that she and Marvin had been taking Steven to Ellen Barfield's old church rather often since Jessica's return to Bisbee.

Suddenly, he realized that the song service had ended, and Steven was tugging at his hand to be seated. Everyone else was already sitting. Acutely aware that people were staring at him curiously, Elliott sat down quickly, his face burning. Maybe he should do his pondering someplace other than church!

As a couple of ushers collected the offering and then a young woman sang, Elliott looked about him, really noticing the church for the first time. It was as small as he remembered from coming here as a child with his mother; it was a little shabbier and badly needed some paint work. The old building probably seated no more than fifty or sixty people but most of the old pews were filled, he observed.

The old man who had been the pastor was gone, of course, and a smooth-faced young man—too young for such a position, Elliott decided sourly—was sitting up front, partially hidden by the pulpit.

An old deacon led in prayer and then turned the pulpit to "Brother Warren, our pastor."

The young pastor stepped to the pulpit—eagerly, it seemed to Elliott. "Please turn to First John, chapter two, verse eleven," he said. "Would you all stand for the reading of God's Word?"

Elliott stood obediently with the others, then drew out his mother's small leather Bible from his coat pocket and began to flip through the pages, searching for the Scripture. He was amazed—and even a little proud—to discover that what he had learned as a child going to Sunday School and church came flooding back, and with comparative ease, he found the Scripture.

As Pastor Warren read the text, Elliott felt a jolt in the pit of his stomach. It was the same verse he had found underlined in his mother's Bible!

"But he that hateth his brother is in darkness, and walketh in darkness, and knoweth not whither he goeth, because that darkness hath blinded his eyes."

"Hate and resentment are a part of the sin nature of man," the pastor's voice rang out clear and serious in the small auditorium. "They are weapons Satan uses against Christians and non-Christians alike. And, unless we are willing to give them up, there is little God can do for us. I know it is easier to tell someone to give up hate and resentment than it is for that person to give them up."

Elliott's eyes were glued to the pastor's face as he continued. "Perhaps someone has hurt you so deeply, or treated you so cruelly, that you find you cannot forgive that person. You may not even want to give up the hate."

The boyish minister paused to survey the people with sympathetic eyes, then he said clearly and forcefully, "But *you* do not have to give it up, just be *willing* to give it up! Jesus Christ has the only 'hate eraser' available and it's yours when you ask Christ to forgive you. Then our wonderful Lord Jesus, who loved us so much that He gave *His* life that *we* might have life, will erase that hate and resentment from our lives as if they were never there!"

"I don't believe that," Elliott muttered to himself. Then he felt hot color wash up his neck into his face. He hadn't meant to speak out loud. He glanced around to see if anyone had heard but saw that every eye was on the minister.

The pastor's face glowed with earnestness. "In Matthew 6, verses fourteen and fifteen, the Bible records Jesus's own words, 'If ye forgive not men their trespasses, neither will your Father forgive your trespasses.'"

Elliott felt hot and then cold. One reason Elliott felt he made a good news reporter was his ability to separate himself from sentimentality. He dealt in facts and facts alone. Yet, since he had come back to Coppercrest, it seemed his mother's words followed him, haunting him and making mush out of him!

"Elliott, please do not hate your father and brother." His eyes again traced the nine words written in his mother's Bible.

Sure he hated Cyrus! He didn't deny it. The only reason he had come here was out of a feeling of debt and the teaching his mother had drilled into him that he must respect Cyrus, regardless of personal feeling, just because Cyrus was his stepfather.

Now this young upstart of a preacher was trying to tell him he must forgive the man, too. Cyrus had not even asked to be forgiven—and would never do so!

But the underlined verse in the Bible he still held in his hand seemed to leap from the page at him.

"He that hateth his brother is in darkness."

Sure, he hated Austin, too. And with good reason! His lips twisted in a bitter smile. So had others—and that was, no doubt, why he was dead.

He shuddered. At least he had not resorted to that extreme. But someone had—and he, Elliott, was not sorry. Austin had deserved what he got!

His mother's words from the margin seemed to reprove him.

"Elliott, please do not hate your father and brother."

He could almost hear her soft voice and see her gentle face, ravaged by sickness but beautiful still—perhaps by the beauty that filled her loving heart.

Was he willing to forgive his stepfather and brother? The answer came as almost a shout in his mind: No, a thousand times no!

Elliott felt the eyes of the pastor were boring into his very soul as he finished softly, "Hate is a corrosive acid that eats away at the soul of man, a poison that taints and pollutes the mind. Hate is a destroyer that not only harms the person who harbors it but wounds and hurts others as well. If you have never accepted Jesus Christ as your personal Savior, you have no defense against the power of this evil in your life. You need to ask Jesus to forgive you and believe in Him as the Son of God who died and rose again. When you ask Him to save you, He washes the past away with all its bitterness and anger. A new life is yours—literally for the asking."

Elliott felt flayed, beaten—and relieved—when the pastor said, "Would everyone please rise? Let us pray."

With his head bowed, at least Elliott could get away from the penetrating eyes of the young minister who seemed to be looking right into his heart.

When the pastor finished his final prayer, he smilingly urged the congregation to assemble together again that evening at seven. "And do come be with us in service next Sunday, also."

"Never!" Elliott muttered to himself as he turned and headed for the door and fresh air. But the pastor's words burned in his heart, flooding it with an intense emotion he could not explain or name.

21

When they arrived home after church, Tilda met them at the door to announce that Sunday dinner was almost ready and that Cyrus wanted Steven to take dinner with the family.

Elliott told Allyssa—who was coming from the family room with Gentry—that he would see to washing Steven's hands for dinner.

When they came down a few minutes later, Elliott saw that Cyrus was at the head of the table and Jessica at the other end, as usual. Gentry usually sat on Cyrus's right, but today there was an empty place on both sides of Cyrus. Gentry was seated farther down the table, across from Allyssa.

"Sit here," Cyrus directed Elliott, indicating the chair on his right. "And, Steven, you are to sit here on my left."

Puzzled by the ceremonial turn this was taking, Elliott glanced at the others as he sat down and saw a frown on Gentry's face. Allyssa met his eyes with a warm light in hers. Something was going on that the others seemed to know—or suspect—but he was completely in the dark.

His mystification deepened when he saw Tilda, John, and Marvin all file in and stand in a row to Cyrus's left. When they were in place, Cyrus beamed upon the assembled members of the house like a monarch upon his court.

"I know everyone is hungry, so I won't make this long," Cyrus announced. He turned to Steven. "As you all know, Steven—as my heir through my son, Austin—will someday be the head of Gypsy Blue Enterprises."

His eyes swung from the wide-eyed gaze of his grandson to Elliott. "And you all know by now that Elliott, my stepson, owns a fourth interest in Gypsy Blue Enterprises. But what you don't know is that Elliott had consented to be Steven's guardian. So, to help him fulfill his duties more effectively, I am making him Vice-President of Gypsy Blue Enterprises."

Smoothly, he turned to Gentry. "Of course, you will still be my General Manager, Gentry, but from now on you will take your orders from Elliott, as well as from me. Elliott will hold the office Austin held when he died."

There was dead silence in the room for a full moment. Elliott saw a flush of hot blood rise in Gentry's face and for a moment it looked like he might explode. The look he gave to Elliott before he dropped his eyes was murderous. He took a deep breath and said in low tones, "Whatever you say, Mr. Barfield."

Elliott saw Tilda look at Gentry, then saw tears fill her eyes before she looked down. John looked completely unperturbed.

Lee stood as if she were not even a part of the scene. But her eyes were busy, Elliott saw, searching the faces and actions of the persons in the room.

Elliott lifted a protesting hand. "I–I know you mean well, sir, but I have no desire to be a part of Gypsy Blue Enterprises. I know nothing about the business and don't want to learn. When my business is over here, I plan to go back to my work."

"We will talk more about that later," Cyrus interrupted. "And for now, that is the way it is. I have had papers drawn up to that effect." He smiled, something he rarely did, and let out a deep breath of satisfaction. "Now, let us eat this wonderful meal the best cook in the country has prepared for us!"

The meal was a quiet and uncomfortable one. In his room, Steven probably would not have talked a great deal, but here, he spoke not at all. Gentry didn't talk at first either, but Cyrus seemed determined to draw him out of his shell, asking questions about his recent trip.

John and Marvin had been dismissed, and Tilda moved in

and out of the dining room without a smile. *Why did the announcement strike Gentry and Tilda so hard?* Elliott wondered. Certainly the vice-presidency would be logical since Elliott was a part owner and Steven's uncle.

Then he remembered that Gentry had been badgering Cyrus to appoint him Steven's guardian. As Steven's guardian, Gentry would have had full control of Gypsy Blue Enterprises when Cyrus died...and the old man was in extremely poor health.

Now, Elliot had come back to Coppercrest and had been pushed into that coveted slot. Even Gentry's girlfriend had been transferring her attention to him. Elliott felt a glacial chill envelop him. He felt sorry for Gentry, but the man was like a wounded bear—dangerous, unpredictable. Perhaps he was Austin's murderer! Could he want control enough to try to kill Cyrus's stepson and grandson, too?

I named it well! Elliott thought uneasily. Deadly Gypsy Blue was appropriate for Gypsy Blue Enterprises. She seemed to be just that to those who loved her.

Allyssa tried valiantly to salvage the dinner with her bright chatter and laughter. Elliott applauded her efforts silently and tried to respond to the remarks she cast his way. Even Gentry and Cyrus seemed appreciative of her efforts. But Jessica remained silent, as if lost in her own little world.

Elliott sensed that everyone was glad when the meal was over. He told Allyssa he would put Steven to bed for a nap and escaped as quickly as possible.

Back in their rooms, and stretched on his own bed, Steven begged for a story, but Elliott was glad the child was asleep before he had read two pages. He locked the door to Steven's room and tiptoed into his own room, locking the hall door there.

Taking his mother's little Bible from his jacket pocket, Elliott walked out onto the little deck and stretched out in a lounge chair. His nerves were strung so tightly he felt he could almost hear them hum, like high powerline wires. The air was fresh and cool and smelled of honeysuckle. He lay very still and some of the quietness of his surroundings began to seep into his troubled spirit.

A tiny brown hummingbird darted down to sip at first one flower and then another, totally ignoring Elliott's still form. A large, blue, incredibly beautiful butterfly flitted onto the deck and settled on the rim of a glass of water Elliott had left on the table yesterday. For a breathtaking moment she trembled there, not more than a couple of feet from Elliott's face. Then she rose like a puff of thistledown and capered from blossom to blossom on the honeysuckle vine.

Propping his head up with a pillow, Elliott opened the Bible. Suddenly, he wanted to know if his mother had written other notes to him. Even if they caused him pain, it made her feel close to him again. He could almost hear her talking to him when he saw the well-remembered handwriting.

The pages were worn and yellowed, he noticed as he began to leaf through the book of Matthew. Suddenly, his heart seemed to stop beating. In the margin of a page, Elliott found another brief note to him. Elliott's heart began to pound as he read the few words:

"Elliott, I am praying for you right now as I read. And I claim this rest from God's Word for you."

Beside the brief note a few words were underlined:

"Come unto me, all ye that labour and are heavy laden, and I will give you rest."

Elliott could feel again the acute loneliness and rejection he had known as a child in this house.

"Yes, Mother," Elliott muttered, "there were times when I desperately needed rest from my pain here at Coppercrest. I wonder why you didn't leave this place and take me with you? But I suppose you loved Cyrus, and certainly you loved Austin. Maybe you didn't know how bad things were for me here."

He had tried to shield his mother from unpleasantness of any kind, leaving all of it outside the room she had seldom left the last several years of her life.

He turned the pages idly and discovered that other pages had little notes to him. He read them hungrily. Then he found one that was addressed to Cyrus and he read it curiously:

"Cyrus, Cyrus, if only you would heed this verse! I fear for your soul, if you do not."

The words that were underlined widened Elliott's eyes. It was the same verse that had popped from Elliott's mouth in his stepfather's presence on Friday!

"For what is a man profited, if he shall gain the whole world, and lose his own soul?"

Elliott chuckled softly. "I should show him what Mother wrote to him, and this verse," he said. "He would probably never admit the verse meant Cyrus Barfield!"

He continued to turn the pages, stopping to read the little notes when, suddenly, one caught his attention:

"This is for you, Elliott," his mother had written. "I tried to teach you the Scriptures. Please allow them to make you wise unto salvation."

He felt a tightening in his throat as he read the verse in II Timothy that was underlined:

"And that from a child thou hast known the holy scriptures, which are able to make thee wise unto salvation through faith which is in Christ Jesus."

It was true. Mother had read him—and Austin—a Bible story each night before they went to bed. He had mostly enjoyed just hearing her read to him. He could still hear her saying to Austin and him, "Jesus didn't have to die for His own sins because He didn't have any. He died for our sins, boys. Yours and mine and for all the people of the world."

"But look what your God did for you!" Elliott suddenly said aloud, so savagely that the little brown hummingbird bounced into the air and streaked away. "Your God let you die when He could have healed you like He healed people in those stories you told us from the Bible. If He loved you, why didn't He heal you?"

His fingers flipped several pages and suddenly his eyes saw a note that made a quiver run down his backbone. He could almost hear her gentle voice speaking the words written there in the margin beside two underlined verses in the fifth chapter of James.

"I want to be well—my boys need me—but I know God cares for them even more than I do. He's in control. And this I do know: I'm a child of God and when I wake up in heaven, I will never have a sick body again."

A tremendous longing rose in Elliott's heart. "But I don't know how to get what you had, Mother!"

Elliott rose and paced the deck, a sadness and uneasiness heavy upon his spirit. "I wish I had never come back here," he said fiercely. "Mother has become more real to me, and now I'm tied to Gypsy Blue Enterprises. The power and luxuries are worthless! I have never been so miserable!"

Ever since the mower incident, a sense of impending danger had weighed upon him. Could that account for his deep unhappiness and unrest? The little notes in his mother's handwriting had at first brought a sense of his mother's presence and then an almost unbearable longing. He missed her more now than he had in several years. But something was eating away at him—and between his mother's God and the foreboding sense of something about to happen, he didn't know what to do.

22

A nightmare of climbing endless stone stairways through a murky darkness with voices pursuing him filled Elliott's sleep. The word "darkness" was repeated over and over, echoing hollowly like it was bouncing off the walls of a long tunnel or canyon.

Elliott stumblingly climbed and climbed the cold stone stairway in eerie darkness, fleeing from the voices until his limbs were so weak he could scarcely crawl up the next step. He could hear his hoarse and labored breathing and there was a pain like fire in his chest.

Then something was pounding on his chest. He raised his arms to ward off the blows, and heard Steven's frightened voice. "Uncle Elliott! Uncle Elliott! Wake up! Wake up!"

Elliott snapped awake and sat up. In the dim light of a night light, he could see Steven's small figure standing beside his bed. His face was pale with fright.

"Are—are you all right, Uncle Elliott?" Steven quavered.

Elliott reached over and switched on a lamp beside his bed and sighed with deep relief. The light was so wonderful after the horror of fleeing endlessly in that terrible darkness.

"Yeah, I'm all right—and thanks for rescuing me from that awful nightmare! You're a real pal." Elliott ran his hand through his hair and his fingers came away wet. He glanced down and saw that his pillow was wet with sweat—and maybe a few tears, he thought wryly.

"I—I woke up and heard you moaning," Steven said, his

small face earnest. "I–I thought you might be sick. I called but you didn't come awake, so I finally pounded you on the chest. The—the sounds you were making s–scared me."

"And you did right!" Elliott said, reaching over and taking one of Steven's small hands in his large one. The child's hand was cold.

"C–can I get in bed with you? For a little bit?" Steven asked hesitantly. "I–I'm still kinda s–scared."

"Sure thing, little guy," Elliott said. "And don't you worry, I'm all right now. I just had a crazy old nightmare!"

Steven bounced into bed and snuggled his small head down in the crook of Elliott's arm. His hair felt silky against Elliott's bare arm. He felt a tightening of his throat and drew Steven close. The little boy sighed and snuggled closer.

A rare kind of peace stole over Elliott as he lay very still and listened to the breathing of his small nephew grow steady and deep. Whatever tomorrow brought, this fragile boy-child of his hated brother needed him, and he planned to be there for him.

Elliott awoke to a soft tap at his door. The room was flooded with sunlight. Raising his head, he saw Steven was still deep in sleep, pressed close to Elliott's side. Something about the tousled, light-brown head and the silky eyelashes resting on Steven's pale cheeks brought back the strange but heady feeling of the night before.

Rolling gently away from the child, Elliott climbed from bed and grabbed a robe, putting it on as he went to the door. When he opened it, he saw Allyssa standing there, a smile on her face.

"Aren't you two up yet?" she asked lightly. "It's nine-thirty. You haven't even had breakfast, and it's almost time for Steven's lessons."

"I guess we slept in," Elliott said. "Do you suppose Tilda will still give us something to eat?" His tone was bantering. He realized that he felt good this morning—at peace with himself and the world. He smiled at the picture Allyssa made. Wearing a pale green linen-like dress, her gold hair drawn back and pinned with a large green velvet bow in back, her gentle expression made him feel even happier.

"How about going for a drive after breakfast?" Elliott asked suddenly. "We could drive across the border into Mexico and do a little shopping."

"What about Steven's lessons?" Allyssa said hesitantly.

"Let the lessons go for today," Elliott said recklessly. "Remember," he added teasingly, "your boss said you were also to take orders from me."

Delight danced in Allyssa's eyes. "Okay, boss, if you say so! A drive it is—in your handsome Porsche, I presume."

"Naturally!"

Allyssa's smile was warm as she said gaily, "I'll help Steven get ready while you go scare up some breakfast for you two."

Elliott moved back into the room. "Go on over to Steven's room, and I'll send him in to you. I've got to get some clothes on. Tilda would never approve of me running about the halls in my robe and pajamas."

Allyssa started to move to Steven's door, then stopped abruptly. She turned to Elliott with dismay written on her face.

"I can't go, Elliott," she said, her blue-grey eyes filled with regret. "Yesterday I promised Gentry I would go with him to Tucson this afternoon. After his business appointment, he is taking me to dinner and then to a theater performance he's been wanting me to see. I'm so sorry."

"Oh. Well, that's okay," Elliott said. "We'll go another time."

Allyssa nodded and turned away. But Elliott's heart did a couple of flip-flops. Allyssa would rather have gone with him than Gentry!

Elliott found it was not as difficult to spend time with Steven as he had thought it would be. Monday and Tuesday, he and Steven walked around town. The child had gone almost nowhere in his short life and the commonest trip was an adventure. Wednesday, Gentry took Elliott to visit the Gypsy Blue Mine, and Steven was in ecstasies that he was allowed to go.

Elliott was touched by Steven's obvious hunger for love when Elliott showed him any attention at all. And ever since the night of Elliott's nightmare, Steven had become almost possessive about him.

When Elliott noticed the child's adoring eyes on him, he felt a quickening in his heart and a familiar tightening of his throat. No one but his mother had ever really loved him, Elliott felt, and he remembered the painful hunger for affection and approval he had known as a child.

And, although he had not asked Allyssa to go out again, she had shown in a dozen little ways that she found his presence enjoyable.

Tilda had apparently cast off her moodiness and was her old cheerful self again, baking him special things as she had always done when he was a child. Even Gentry seemed to accept him in his new position. Although he was not jovial or warm toward Elliott, he treated him with polite and respectful deference.

The only strange note of the week came when his mother's Bible disappeared again on Monday after he had attended church on Sunday. At first he thought he might have misplaced it, but when he searched his room and didn't find it, he decided someone had taken it again. Deeply annoyed, he told the other members of the household about its loss but no one seemed to know anything about it—or no one admitted anything.

Although he felt the loss keenly, he could come up with no logical reason why anyone would want his mother's old Bible.

The only other jarring note in the rather satisfying week came on Friday when the police chief called.

"If you know for certain Lee Barfield wrote the note you received about your letter at the post office, then you can be equally sure she wrote the others, too. The same person wrote them all!" he told Elliott emphatically.

Incensed at the deception, Elliott immediately accosted Lee in the chauffeur's little apartment. "You lied to me," Elliott told her angrily, informing her curtly of what the police chief had said.

For a moment, Elliott thought Lee was going to deny it, but then she slumped down on the bed and said in defeated tones, "Okay, he's right. I did write all the notes."

Looking up at Elliott, her eyes filled with tears, "I–I knew that the notes were a stupid thing—so I lied to you about them."

"Why did you write notes threatening to kidnap Steven and even hinting you might harm him?" Elliott demanded.

"I–I thought they might stir things up—and I might discover who really did kill Austin. But I see now that it just makes me look more guilty."

"Because you did kill Austin, didn't you?"

"No! I swear I did not!"

"Just like you swore you didn't write those other notes?" Elliott said coldly.

"I know it was dumb to lie about them—just as dumb as it was to write them—but I still didn't kill my husband!... W–What are you going to do?" she asked through trembling lips.

"I don't know," Elliott said more gently, softening a little.

"Please, give me a little time," Lee pleaded. "We must find out something soon that will help clear me. Steven isn't in any danger from me. You know I would never harm him. Besides, you are with him almost constantly."

She finished on a bitter note. "You don't even allow me any time alone with him anymore."

"And I won't until we have clear evidence you had nothing to do with Austin's death," Elliott said sternly. "However, I won't turn you over to the police yet. But, I'm breaking the law, and this can't go on indefinitely."

"I know, and I'm grateful. Please, help me find Austin's killer," Lee whispered.

Elliott nodded slowly, but within twenty-four hours, he bitterly regretted his decision.

23

The next morning around eleven o'clock, Allyssa called Elliott. He had barely put the receiver to his ear when she began to sob hysterically. Between deep gulps, she gasped out, "Elliott, Marvin k–kidnapped S–Steven!"

Horror like he had never known before shook Elliott to the core of his heart. For a moment, shock held him utterly speechless. Finally, the words rushed out, "How could that happen? You didn't leave him alone with Marvin, did you? You had specific orders to stay with him every minute!"

Allyssa seemed to be struggling to control her voice and finally choked out, "No, of course I didn't leave him alone with Marvin—since you told me not to! Steven was taking his piano lesson, so I ran down to the variety store and left him in the care of the piano teacher. I wasn't gone ten minutes, I know."

"I can't believe you would leave the child!" Elliott knew his accusing voice strongly resembled his stepfather's tones but he didn't care. Nothing mattered at the moment but Steven!

"I'm so s–sorry, Elliott. I guess I didn't really believe he was in any real danger. And I–I was gone such a short time! When I got back, Janet, his piano teacher, seemed surprised to see me. She said I had only been gone a couple of minutes when Marvin came to the door and said I had suddenly taken very sick and he wanted to collect Steven so he could take me home immediately."

"How do you know it was Marvin who took him? Does the piano teacher know Marvin?"

"Not really, but the man said he was the chauffeur, and he certainly fit her description of Marvin, the same height and build, brown hair and beard, dark blue eyes."

"Have you called the police?"

"Yes! I'm at the police station now. The police are already out looking for Marvin and the Barfield car."

"I'll be right there! I don't think I'll tell Cyrus yet. Maybe they'll get Steven back immediately. And—Allyssa, I'm sorry I was so—so harsh. I'm just upset."

"I know, Elliott. But I do blame myself. How could I have left Steven after you warned me not to...."

"It's okay! I'll see you as soon as I can get there!"

When Elliott tore into the police station a few minutes later, he saw Allyssa sitting wretchedly in a corner of the room. Her face was pale and her eyes slightly swollen from crying. She was twisting a handkerchief to shreds.

When he entered, she jumped to her feet and ran to him. Her lovely face registered anguish and pain.

Elliott put his arm around her and asked quickly, "Have they found Steven yet?"

"No, but they have Marvin. They said he was up at Castlerock—you know that huge boulder that sticks up from the hillside in one part of town."

Drawing Allyssa with him, Elliott approached the desk. An officer came quickly toward him and spoke respectfully, "I'm Police Chief Charles Richter. You must be Mr. Barfield's stepson. Miss Star said you were coming."

"Yes, I'm Elliott Fleet," Elliott said tersely. "Allyssa said you have Marvin. Has he told you where Steven is?"

"No, I'm afraid not," the police chief said. "He denies any knowledge of the child's disappearance. Said he knew the boy would be taking a lesson for an hour, so he went up to Castlerock to do a little sketching."

The police officer laughed harshly. "But we know he took the boy. He had parked the car on the road below and when we searched it, we found one of the child's shoes. The ones Miss Star said he was wearing today!"

The officer's mouth tightened into a straight, grim line and he laughed shortly. "That wasn't the biggest surprise." The chief hesitated for a second, then said, "I expect you don't know that your chauffeur is not a man, after all! When we shook him down for weapons, we discovered Marvin Maxell is a woman—and none other than Lee Barfield, the child's mother! The police in 50 states have been looking for her, and she was under my nose all the time!"

"No!" Elliott heard himself exclaiming.

Allyssa gasped and exclaimed in horror, "Marvin Maxell is Lee Barfield? That's incredible! How could he be Lee Barfield? I've seen videos of Lee, and he looks nothing like her!"

"I know," Chief Richter said. "I remember Lee Barfield, too, from the trial and all." He shook his head in disbelief. "I didn't recognize her at first, even without the beard. But when I saw her face—in spite of having slimmed down and with dark blue contacts—I remembered her. She has a face a person doesn't forget easily."

"Could I talk to her?" Elliott asked.

"Well—we're far from finished with her ourselves," the officer demurred.

"She's my sister-in-law," Elliott said, "maybe I can get something from her you can't. I'd like to try. Alone, if you don't mind."

"Well, okay, give it your best shot. So far, she has refused to say anything to us, except for denying she took Steven. Won't even admit to being Lee Barfield."

Allyssa volunteered to go with Elliott, but he insisted on seeing her alone.

Elliott was taken through a locked door and then down a long corridor to the end cell. Lee was lying on a metal bunk with her head on her arms. She lifted her head when Elliott entered. The cell door was locked after him.

Elliott felt a jolt when he looked into Lee's face—minus the beard. The resemblance between Steven and his mother was unnerving. The same slim, triangular face, the same dark eyelashes and eyebrows. Her eyes were a copper-flecked, gold-hazel now, without the contacts, and Steven's were grey, but they were both slightly slanted.

In spite of the chauffeur uniform which she still wore, Lee looked fully feminine. Her slim brown hands were twisted in her lap as she sat up, and her eyes looked haunted.

As soon as the police officer left them, Lee jumped up and spoke in a voice ragged with pain—Lee's husky voice that he remembered, "Elliott, you have to help me! I didn't kidnap Steven! Someone else has him and they may kill him! Just as they killed his father."

Elliott felt many emotions struggling together in his mind: anger and pity, unbelief wrestling with belief, desperate fear for Steven...and frustration.

"Lee," he said sternly, "you must tell me the truth. The police found one of Steven's shoes in the car you were driving. One of the shoes he was wearing this morning! How do you account for that?"

"You've got to believe me, Elliott! Someone must have put Steven's shoe in the car after he was kidnapped. It would have been easy! I parked the car on the street below and walked up the hill to Castlerock—for the exercise."

"How can I believe you?" Elliott said impatiently. "You lied to me about the notes. The piano teacher described the man who took Steven. The description fits you exactly! Steven's shoe was found in the car.

"Lee, why don't you tell me the truth? If you will, I promise to do all I can to help you. Get you a good lawyer—anything! Just tell me where Steven is—please!"

For a long moment Lee stared at Elliott with agony in her eyes. When she spoke, despair filled her voice. "Can't you see what's happening? Someone is trying to make it look like I kidnapped Steven—just like someone framed me for Austin's murder. Can't you see?"

"I only know that Steven has been kidnapped," Elliott said doggedly. "I've got to find him! Cyrus could have a stroke when he finds out he's missing. I'm responsible for him—and—I've grown very fond of him."

His voice broke, and Elliott felt hot tears well up suddenly in his eyes. He hadn't cried since his mother died! Turning away from Lee, he dashed the tears from his eyes with his coat sleeve.

He felt Lee's hand on his arm and turned back to her. She stood close to him, and her whole soul was in her eyes as she said softly, "Elliott, I'm thankful you care about Steven. His father never did—nor does his grandfather. To them, he is just a twig on their family tree that will grow up to care for and nurture the real love of their lives—Gypsy Blue Enterprises."

She looked away and suddenly her face hardened. She said harshly, "How I hate that business! If it had not been for it, perhaps Austin and I might have gone away from his father and made a go of our marriage. But Austin would never have left Gypsy Blue!"

She swung back to Elliott, and the grip on his arm tightened until he winced.

She lifted tragic, copper-flecked eyes to Elliott's and spoke urgently, "Elliott, you are my only hope—and Steven's. Please find my son! I'd be willing to go back to prison if I knew he was safe. Oh, please find him, Elliott; someone means to kill him. I feel it in my heart. Please find Steven before it's forever too late!"

24

Elliott didn't let his stepfather know of Steven's disappearance for a couple of hours. But when an intensive search by the police department, the sheriff's department and many volunteers, plus Elliott and Allyssa failed to find the child, he had to notify Cyrus.

Cyrus, as Elliott had known he would, went into a blind rage, blaming the piano teacher, Allyssa, and everyone else. But he berated Elliott without mercy.

"I told you to not let the child out of your sight," he stormed. "And you let one woman outsmart you! You—or someone in this stupid household—should have seen through Lee's deceitful disguise! If I could get my hands on that woman, I'd tear her limb from limb!"

"We don't know for certain that Lee did this," Elliott said as gently as he could.

"Of course she did! The police have her in custody, don't they? Steven's shoe was found in the car he—she—was driving, wasn't it?"

"Cyrus," Elliott said, "if someone *was* trying to frame Lee, it would have been easy to plant the shoe in the car. Lee swears she didn't kidnap the boy!"

Cyrus exploded in rage, almost choked, and finally managed to sputter, "And you believe her? You are an absolute fool! Just like you always were! I should have known better than to bring you here to protect my grandson! You don't have the sense you were born with! Never did and never will have!"

Cyrus ran out of breath and his hoarse breathing sounded erratic and harsh over the phone line. Elliott thought that his stepfather would suffer a stroke if he continued like this. And at this moment, he wouldn't care if he did!

Elliott took several deep breaths before he could answer calmly and rationally. He felt like ranting and raving back, but he refused to give in to the temptation. Steven was the only thing that mattered now.

"I didn't say I believed Lee," Elliott said finally. "She could be guilty, but we need to look at every possibility. Above everything right now, we need to find Steven."

Cyrus had gathered enough breath to talk again. "Lee is trying to get even with me," he raved bitterly. "When I testified against her, her eyes on me were burning with hate. If she could have reached me, I'm sure she would have torn me to pieces with claws and teeth!"

"If Lee has kidnapped Steven, I can't believe she would let any harm come to him," Elliott said. "He's her son and she loves him."

"The woman is insane," Cyrus growled. "As crazy as a loon! You should have heard her stand up and scream like a she-cat when she was convicted of murdering Austin. She was all but foaming at the mouth, shrieking that she had been framed and that everyone was against her. Then she collapsed and practically had to be carried out."

"Who wouldn't have gone a bit crazy, if she was convicted for a crime she didn't do?"

"Are you taking up for that crazy woman?" Cyrus asked incredulously. His voice rose almost to a shriek. "She killed your brother!"

"He was never a brother to me!"

"And I'm sure you are glad he's dead! You hated Austin, just like a lot of other people!" Cyrus shouted. "Maybe you were the one who killed him, if Lee didn't!"

For a moment Elliott was too shocked to speak, then he began to laugh. The accusation was so absurd, so ludicrous, that it set him off, and he couldn't seem to stop laughing.

He heard his stepfather gasp and then there was utter silence on the other end of the line. Elliott tried to choke off his unrestrained mirth but could not.

Finally he heard Cyrus's voice on the line: curt, cold and commanding, "That will do, Elliott."

That put an instant end to Elliott's laughter, to his vast relief. Wiping the tears from his eyes, Elliott realized that Cyrus also seemed to have taken himself in hand and was once more in control of his emotions.

"What can we do now?" Cyrus asked as calmly as if he had not been throwing slurs and accusations just seconds before.

"We'll work with the police as closely as possible. They're going to keep at Lee and I will, too. I'm going over now to question the piano teacher and the neighbors. I don't plan to leave this strictly up to the police. They have other cases, but Steven is our only concern."

Cyrus cleared his throat and Elliott was amazed to hear him say coldly, "I–I should not have said those things to you. I apologize." Before a bewildered Elliott could frame an answer, his stepfather hung up.

But in spite of all the efforts of the police and Elliott, they learned nothing of Steven's whereabouts. It was as if he had dropped from the face of the earth. No one had seen the child after he left the piano teacher's home.

Late that night, when Elliott returned to Coppercrest, deeply discouraged and tired to the bone, Allyssa met him in the foyer. Her eyes were dark with worry, and the strain was etched on her lovely face. Her voice was pained. "Steven hasn't been found, has he?"

When Elliott wearily shook his head, her expressive eyes clouded with tears as she took his hand in her soft one. "It's all my fault. I am so sorry, Elliott. I will never forgive myself for not taking better care of Steven."

Her voice broke and she dropped her eyes. Elliott felt her tears dropping onto his hand. He felt a strong urge to wrap his arms about her shaking shoulders, but Gentry appeared at that moment.

Elliott saw Gentry's eyes stab jealously into his own as he saw Allyssa holding Elliott's hand. Allyssa dropped her hand when she heard Gentry speak, but she didn't move away from Elliott.

"Have the police found out anything?" Gentry asked curtly.

"Not a thing," Elliott said tiredly. "I understand they plan to question Lee through the night. If she really has kidnapped Steven, then the child could be somewhere all alone—unless she has an accomplice, of course."

"That poor little kid," Allyssa said. "When I think of how terrified he must be, I think I could just start screaming and never stop."

Gentry moved to Allyssa and put his arm about her shoulders possessively. "We're all deeply concerned for Steven, Allyssa, but we have to keep our minds in a positive track. We have to believe the boy will be found unhurt."

A sudden, almost overwhelming wave of jealousy flooded through Elliott when Gentry put his arm around Allyssa. A red mist of anger seemed to rise in his mind.

He stepped quickly away from Allyssa and Gentry. What was happening to him? In horror, he realized that an almost unconquerable urge to punch the tender, loving expression from Gentry's face was raging through him. Was he this tired, or was he falling in love with Steven's lovely nanny?

Pleading tiredness, Elliott hastily excused himself and started away. Allyssa's warm voice called after him, "I'll have Tilda bring you something to eat."

Muttering his thanks, Elliott ran upstairs and into the safety of his room. Shakily he slumped into a chair and closed his eyes. Something almost like terror shook him. Was he, Elliott Fleet, the man who had eluded all matrimonial nooses thrown his way, falling for a girl? And for Gentry's girl, at that?

The nightmare came again that night. Climbing endless stone and concrete stairways, through semi-darkness, this time Elliott was searching for Steven, and it was his own voice that echoed through the dim, hollow passageways, calling Steven's name over and over. A small shadowy figure was always climbing above him, but he could never get close enough to see if it was Steven.

His own voice shouting Steven's name finally woke him. The pillow and sheet were wet with his sweat, and he was shaking as if he had a chill. He couldn't go to sleep again, so he got up and walked the floor for awhile.

He finally took a shower, put on dry pajamas and a robe against the night chill, and walked out onto the deck. The air was coolly refreshing and scented with honeysuckle. Bright, white stars sprinkled against the black sky made a sudden catch rise in his throat. The moon rode high, cold and silvery in the huge vault of the sky.

He had always loved the night. Mysterious and serene, it clothed even squalor and ugliness with the richness of silver and velvety blacks and greys.

Leaning on the parapet surrounding the deck, he wondered if Steven liked the night. Or was he afraid of the dark? His throat tightened almost unbearably. He couldn't believe how much he cared for that one little boy. There was so much to show him, so much to teach him! Would he ever see Steven again?

"Dear God! Bring him back to me!" The poignant cry was wrung from lips trembling with pain.

A small voice seemed to speak deep into Elliott, "Why should I? You are not a child of mine."

Elliott tried to shrug off the words as a figment of his distraught mind. He lifted his eyes to the beauty of the sky, and a deep hunger surged into his heart—a longing he had never known. He felt his eyes prickle as a thought slid into his mind: How wonderful it must be to know God intimately—the Creator of beauty—like his mother had known Him!

Deep inside him he seemed to hear words of his mother's that he had long since forgotten. "Son, God made man different from all his other creatures. He gave us a soul and made a special place in each of us that is reserved for Himself. Unless God is allowed to occupy that space, you can never have real peace."

Suddenly, his old excuse that he would never serve the God who took away his mother seemed pettish and childish.

An intense longing gripped his heart until it throbbed with pain. He felt something drop on his hands, clenching the railing of the parapet, and was surprised to see they were tears...his tears. Words tumbled in anguish from his mouth, "Dear God, will you still take me—after all these years of rejecting you?"

Elliott dropped his head in his hands and groaned, "Why should you take me? I've rejected you, scorned you, even when I knew it broke my poor mother's heart. I wouldn't blame you if you turn me away. I deserve it!" Hot tears drenched his hands, and he writhed in his shame and despair.

After a few moments, Elliott straightened and lifted his head to the sky and felt a feather-soft breeze brush his hot, tear-drenched face. The sky seemed hushed, as if it were waiting. Waiting for what? For Elliott Fleet to acknowledge he was a sinner who needed forgiveness?

"Please forgive me, God. I need your Son as my Savior. I believe in Him and in all that your Word says about Him. Forgive me for my sins. Please accept me as your child. I long to know you—and to have your peace."

No thunder rolled nor did lightning flash, but Elliott felt relief flood over him like a welcome summer shower. *I'm a child of God,* he thought, and a fierce joy coursed through his veins like fire.

Suddenly, Elliott tensed. Standing very still, Elliott let his eyes rove all about him. He turned his head slightly to catch the sound better. He was certain now that he heard faint voices. They seemed to float up to him from the bottom of the long, stone stairway.

The steep stone stairs connected Coppercrest above to the Gypsy Blue Enterprises workshops and jewelry store built down below the almost perpendicular slope of a high, rocky promontory.

Elliott looked inside at his digital clock. It was almost 2 a.m. No one should be on the Gypsy Blue property at this time of the morning!

As silent as vapor, Elliott slipped out of his house slippers and descended the stairway. His bare feet sped silently down the stairs. Halfway down, he stopped to listen. The subdued voices came more clearly to him now, but they still were very faint.

When he reached the bottom of the stairs, Elliott found the gate unlocked. He was thankful he had taken on the job of locking it each night, and tonight, in his tiredness, he had forgotten. He hesitated and listened. The voices, low and whispery, came from around the corner of the building a few yards away.

He pushed gently on the gate and was horrified to hear a faint, but audible screech come from it. He held his breath. The voices abruptly ceased, and he heard quick, hurried steps.

Elliott rushed through the gate, leaving it ajar, and sprang to the corner in time to see a dark figure duck into a car parked at the curb in front of the Gypsy Blue building. The engine purred to life and the car raced away into the night.

The parking lot was only dimly lighted, but the car was small and dark. He had only glimpsed the driver, and could not tell if it was male or female.

A movement in the shadows of the darkened building, only faintly illuminated by night lights caught his eye. Elliott turned in time to see a shadowy figure slip into a doorway just a few yards from him. Elliott sprinted toward it. As he grabbed for the doorknob, he heard the gentle click of a bolt being slid into place.

Hesitating only a second, he turned and raced around the corner. Dashing through the gate, he pounded up the stone, ladder-like steps. The person who just entered the door downstairs must have had a key to get into the building and was using the inside elevator. Whoever it was had to be part of the Coppercrest household!

He reached the deck panting and winded, but he didn't pause. Sprinting through his room, he quickly unlocked his door and slid out into the the hall. The house was silent.

He looked up and down the hall. Nothing moved. Moving swiftly on feet which were now stinging from his race up the stone treads outside, he came to the curving stairway and looked down. There was no movement or sound below.

He was about to go back to his room when he heard soft footsteps—muted by the deep pile of the carpet—somewhere downstairs, then the soft click of a door closing. He had been right! One of the people at the clandestine meeting was a member of the Coppercrest household. But whether staff or family member, he had no idea.

Did that meeting have something to do with Steven? If only he knew. A sudden thought brought him abruptly upright. What if Steven had been abducted by someone at Coppercrest—and he was hidden right here?

"Dear Father," Elliott prayed as he slipped into bed a few minutes later, marveling at the word as it came off his lips. "Help us to find Steven. And thank you for showing mercy to me when I deserved no mercy." His last conscious thought was how good it was to know his mother's God at last.

The next morning, as soon as it was light, Elliott sought out Tilda in her large brick and copper kitchen. He briefly told her what had transpired the night before, though not about accepting Christ. "I think we should search Coppercrest," he declared. "What better place to hide the child than in his own home?

Especially if Lee or someone from this household abducted him."

But an hour later, Elliott had to concede that the child was not anywhere at Coppercrest. For good measure, he also searched the workrooms and storerooms in the building below that weren't being used regularly, but Steven was not found.

Discouraged and morose, Elliott went outside the Gypsy Blue building and walked to the curb. It was a cool, delightfully fresh and sunny morning and he would have reveled in it if only Steven were here to enjoy it, too.

Where was the child? Elliott's insides felt like an empty, lonely chasm, hollow and echoing like the stone stairways in his nightmares.

Sordid images of abused, terrified, and butchered children he had seen in his endless search for newspaper stories crowded into his mind. "Dear Father, please don't let any of this happen to our Steven!

"This will never do!" Elliott muttered. "Gentry was right. I must concentrate on the positive."

Shaking his head to clear it of the haunting phantoms, Elliott started to turn around when he saw a small object laying next to the curb. His heart lurched, then began to pound madly when he leaned over and saw what the object was.

It was Steven's shoe! The mate to the one found in the family car that Lee had been driving when Steven was abducted!

25

With his heart pounding in his ears and feeling slightly light-headed, Elliott stared at the shoe. Had it fallen from the car that sped away from the parking lot last night?

It was possible! Or—his mind was racing now with other possibilities—it could mean that Steven was brought here first. No. The workshops and jewelry store were busy places; the child would have been seen. So Steven's shoe must have fallen from that little, dark car last night!

Elliott picked up the shoe and went back into the store. Riding up in the elevator, he quickly located Allyssa and got her confirmation that the shoe was indeed Steven's shoe. He then briefly told her about the incident of the night before, also about his search of the empty rooms in the house and the workrooms and storerooms in the building below.

Next he called Police Chief Richter and filled him in on the night's adventures and about finding the shoe. The chief came out with two of his men and interrogated everyone who lived or worked at Coppercrest, and everyone who worked in the business below, about their whereabouts when Steven's abduction took place. Cyrus was the only one not grilled; he was barely able to function since Steven's kidnapping.

John took the questioning as mildly as he took everything. He had been working about the yards, he said, and he didn't seem greatly perturbed that it was his word alone that verified it. But both Tilda and Gentry were extremely indignant. However, they alibied each other. The Indian silversmiths and other workers could all vouch for each other that they were working when the abduction took place. Only Gentry carried a key to the building.

The two daily housemaids were questioned but clearly were not involved. Jessica was in her quarters alone and had no alibi—"But I had no reason to kidnap my little grandnephew," she said without rancor. And the chief seemed to agree.

Even Elliott was questioned extensively. The chief was polite but insistent. Elliott explained he had been alone most of the morning, first doing calisthenics on his deck and then some quiet reading in his room.

"It's ridiculous to question Elliott," Tilda snorted at the officers. "Elliott was in his room when I called him to the phone when Allyssa telephoned about Steve's disappearance, and he sure wouldn't have had time to kidnap the boy, hide him, and then rush back in that short a time!"

"Perhaps not," Chief Richter said calmly, "but the young man has only been here a short time and I must check out everyone."

Three agonizing days passed but absolutely nothing turned up that would help in finding Steven. The police officers and Elliott questioned neighbors and people all over town about Steven, showing copies of the latest picture of the five-year-old. The newspaper also carried the picture and a plea for anyone who had any information to contact the police. Even a ten thousand dollar reward, promised to anyone who had information leading to the recovery of Steven, failed to elicit any helpful information.

The police chief had predicted a ransom note or call would be made but not even that came. The small, brown-headed heir to the Barfield fortune seemed to have vanished from the face of the earth.

The police had almost admitted defeat in their questioning of Lee Barfield. She was still the number one suspect, but now it seemed that she might have had an accomplice.

Elliott visited Lee every day. Doggedly, he questioned her, asking her to repeat her story over and over, getting her to talk about anything she would, until Lee would lie down on the bed and turn her face to the wall in tears.

Lee visibly lost weight, her gold-hazel eyes lost their lustre and seemed to sink into hollow, darkened sockets. Her slim, expressive face grew haggard with strain.

The police chief seemed concerned for Lee. "That girl will never make it back to prison at this rate," he said. "She hardly touches her food and at night she groans and cries out in her sleep until the other prisoners are complaining.

"I've had two psychiatrists talking with her to see if they consider her unbalanced. They seem undecided. What I've been concerned about is that she may be a mental case and that she stole her little kid, squirreled him away, and now he's starving while we try to get the truth from her. The psychiatrists agree that it could have happened."

"You mean they think she might have abducted the child and then forgot she did it?" Elliott demanded.

"That's right! I remember how she came completely unglued when she was found guilty of her husband's murder. She had to be kept under the care of a psychiatrist for several weeks after that. They even considered her suicidal."

Dismay filled Elliott's heart as he shook his head and left.

A few minutes past midnight on the fourth day after Steven's disappearance, the private telephone line in Elliott's room rang. Elliott, unable to sleep, was out on the deck. Racing into the room, he snatched up the receiver.

The familiar, husky voice of Lee Barfield spoke softly in his ear. "Elliott, are you alone?"

"Yes—yes!"

He could hear deep breathing over the phone—as if Lee had been running. Then she whispered hurriedly and urgently, "Someone broke me out of jail again. I imagine it is a trap but I went ahead with it!"

"Where are you?" Elliott felt his heart pounding with excitement and trepidation.

Lee paused, drew in a deep, agitated breath and rushed on, without answering his question. "They left me a car. A note was on the seat. It said Steven was imprisoned in the Gypsy Blue Mine. I—I was instructed to go to the mine alone—but I'm frightened. You—you are the only one I even halfway trust."

"I'll come with you," Elliott said quickly. "Should I come in my car?"

"No! I'll be at the foot of the stone stairway, down next to the Gypsy Blue buildings, as quick as I can get there. I'm not far away. Bring a weapon, if you have one, and a flashlight."

The line went dead.

Elliott grabbed his khaki jacket and a large flashlight, then fumbled in a drawer for a box of shells and the small gun he kept there. Grateful now for the dangerous work he did which required him to carry a gun for protection and emergencies, he strapped on his shoulder holster, slipping the weapon in place and put on his jacket. He felt in his pants pocket to be sure his pocketknife was there.

Then, securing his inside door, he dashed out on the deck. Leaving the door unlocked, he leaped down the stone steps. His crepe-soled shoes made little noise on the stone treads but he slowed when he neared the gate. Silently, he unlocked the gate, slid through, and left it unlocked. If he needed to go back up in a hurry, he wanted every advantage possible. Lee had said she might be walking into a trap—but there was also the distinct possibility that she was laying one for him.

Cat-footing it swiftly to the corner of the building, Elliott peered around. The moon was obscured by clouds, but in the dim parking lot light, he could see a car parked at the cub. He could hear the soft purr of its running engine.

His muscles tensed, and he drew in his breath sharply. The car was small—and dark in color. Like the car that had rendezvoused with someone the night after Steven was kidnapped!

A voice almost at his elbow spoke his name softly. He started violently and his hand automatically shot inside his coat.

"It's Lee! Don't shoot me," she whispered. "Come quickly. The police could discover I'm gone at any moment!"

Placing her slim, strong hand on his arm, she looked all around and then drew him swiftly to the car.

"I'll drive," she said hurriedly, slipping into the driver's seat.

Lee had the car in motion before Elliott had his door closed. She drove swiftly through the darkened streets, then out onto the road that led up the canyon toward the Gypsy Blue Mine. It was only three miles to the mine but Elliott's strained nerves seemed to scream for the curvy road to end.

After a few minutes, Lee flicked a quick glance at Elliott and said firmly, "Perhaps you should get down so it will appear that I'm alone."

Elliott slid down on the floorboards until his head couldn't be seen from outside. His long legs were soon extremely uncomfortable.

"Who let you out of jail?" he asked.

"I don't know," Lee said. "That's what worries me. It's just like when I escaped prison. A note was dropped in my cell—by a guard, I guess—after lights-out was called. A man's voice spoke out in the corridor, and I got up and found the note on the floor."

"With the instructions for breaking out?"

"Yes, and that a dark blue Toyota would be parked in the alley behind the jail with the keys in it. It said that my door would be open at fifteen minutes till twelve. I was to go to the left in the hallway and through a door to the outside."

"You never saw anyone?"

"Not a soul. I never even heard anyone open the door but when I checked it at 11:45, it was open. So was the outer door. I was scared to death that it was a trap and that someone would be waiting outside in the alley to shoot me down. But no one was there. Just this car."

Elliott quickly told her about hearing voices and investigating the night of the kidnapping. "I'm almost sure this was the same car," Elliott said.

"That doesn't sound good," Lee said worriedly. "If only we knew if a friend or enemy is letting me out of jail. If it's an enemy, we may not live to get out of this! You know that, don't you? I suppose I was selfish to enlist your help. But if Steven really is in the mine, I knew the chances of freeing him would be greater if you were along."

"Exactly what did the note tell you?" Elliott asked.

"Not much. It's there on the seat," Lee said. "You can read it yourself."

Elliott read the short note by the light of his flashlight. It was printed crudely in pencil on a plain sheet of tying paper:

"Your son is hidden in the old worked-out area of Gypsy Blue Mine. Go alone. A dark blue Toyota will be parked in the alley at the back of jail. Your cell door will be open at fifteen till 12:00 tonight. Go left down the hall. Door will be open. Tell no one!"

"I agree with you," Elliott said when he finished. "It's probably a trap. Yet, what can we do but take any chance that comes along to rescue Steven. We may not get another!"

Silently, he begged the Lord to give them wisdom—and His protection—as they sped through the dark toward what he was very much afraid was a death trap.

26

When Lee swung the car into the parking lot at Gypsy Blue Mine, the building and the entrance to the mine were clearly visible under the large mercury floodlights. Lee coasted into a parking place in front of the building and sat with the engine running for a couple of minutes while they studied the grounds for any movement.

"Just keep the motor running while I check the doors of the building," Elliott directed. "I'm glad I insisted on having a key to things out here. I may want to look inside the building."

Lee nodded mutely, her face pale and her thin body, clad in beige jail clothes, tense.

But after Elliott had gone completely around the building and checked briefly inside, he reported there was no one there.

"Unless someone is hidden behind the big rocks on the mountainsides," Lee said uneasily. "Shall we go inside the mine? Do you have a key to that, too?"

Elliott held up another key in answer, but there was no need to use it. The heavy padlock on the ponderous, iron-grated door hung open.

Lee had found a flashlight in the glove compartment of the car, so each had a light as they moved cautiously and quietly through the iron gate. Elliott took off the padlock and hid it under a large ledge inside the entrance. "So someone won't get the bright idea to lock us in," he told Lee.

Flashing their lights about, they saw no sign of life inside the mine shaft.

Silently, they walked down the narrow mine-car tracks of the tunnel. Elliott tried to not notice how closely the walls—no more than six feet wide most places—pressed in upon them. The walls were irregular and the ceiling curved into a rough arch not far above their heads. Heavy timbers braced the ceiling here and there. A thin trickle of water muddied a tiny ditch beside the tracks.

The shaft widened out into a small room.

"The old workings are down that drift, to our left," Elliott said softly. Another shaft meandered off ahead—like a rabbit-hole—into the darkness. "They only work in here a day or two a month," he added. "And only down that shaft ahead. Then one has to climb up a ladder to the stope, or room, they are working in. Gentry brought me out here a while back and gave me a personally-guided tour."

"I don't like this place," Lee said with a shudder. "It's cold and spooky in here. It must be terrifying for Steven if he is in here."

They walked a short way down the left-hand tunnel until they came to a widened out place that contained a rough desk and bench. "That's where the mine boss made out his reports," Elliott whispered. "Just beyond here we will have to climb a ladder to the stope. If Steven isn't there, we will climb another ladder to the next level."

"Maybe we shouldn't talk anymore unless it's necessary," Lee suggested.

"Good idea."

A few yards farther, Elliott aimed the beam of his light up a vertical ladder on the wall and began to climb. When he came out into a high-vaulted, rough-walled room, he flashed his light around. Steven was not here, he saw with a sinking heart.

Lee stepped off the ladder and looked around. "Where's the next room?" she whispered.

"Down that drift a ways and then up another ladder,"

Elliott whispered, probing the entrance to another rocky shaft with his light.

They moved down the narrow tunnel, following the tracks. Pushing back the blackness with their two flashlights, they walked carefully to keep from falling on the narrow rails sticking up from the gravel and dirt floor. After a few minutes, another ladder appeared on the side of the rough wall.

"Turn out your flashlight for a minute," Elliott whispered, as he flicked his off. "Give me your hand."

As soon as the lights were off, the darkness became absolute. Elliott was acutely aware, then, of the heavy, musty-smelling air, the closeness of the irregular rock walls and ceilings, the puniness of the heavy beam supports. Tons of rock lay above them!

Lee clung tightly to his hand and, suddenly, for the first time, he was aware of her as a woman. She was afraid!

"I thought there might be a light on somewhere if Steven is here," Elliott explained, squeezing her hand reassuringly.

"Let's climb the ladder," Lee said softly. "Then if we don't find him up there somewhere, we can come back and go down this shaft farther."

They switched the lights back on, and Lee drew her hand away, starting up the rough, wooden ladder. Elliott followed. They came out into a small stope. Their lights revealed nothing except more rocks and another ladder.

Lee started toward the ladder, then suddenly stopped and gripped Elliott's arm. "Listen!"

Elliott also stood still but could hear nothing. "Are you sure you heard something?"

"I–I think so. It sounded like faint footsteps. I couldn't tell what direction they were coming from. But now I don't hear anything. Maybe it was just the patter of rat's feet."

The hair on Elliott's neck prickled. He could imagine eyes staring at them from below and from the darkness beyond the top of the ladder—not just rat's eyes! Uneasily, he swung the beam of his light toward the ladder they had just climbed. There was nothing visible there.

"Let's try not to make any noise," Elliott whispered.

Elliott reached for Lee's hand. It felt like a chunk of ice!

Treading lightly, they approached the ladder. Dropping her hand, Elliott shone the light up into the opening. He saw no movement nor heard any sounds. Soundlessly, Elliott stepped onto the ladder rungs and started up with Lee right behind.

As he stepped out in the next stope, Elliott saw that this room was longer. It curved around and disappeared around a corner. Cautiously, he moved aside so Lee could step out onto the slightly uneven floor.

"Switch off your light for a second," Elliott said softly.

In the total darkness, to their left where the room made the turn, a faint light appeared. They stood very still, listening. For a moment there was complete silence, and then a soft sound drifted to them from the left where the light was. Though indistinct and faint, it was unmistakably a sob.

"It's Steven," Lee whispered hoarsely and lunged forward, but Elliott gripped her hand and forcibly held her back.

"We mustn't do anything rash. We're probably heading into a trap," he said softly, but urgently. "So let's be quiet and listen for a few minutes."

If only I knew for certain that it isn't Lee setting a trap for me, he thought. *Then, at least, I wouldn't have to keep my eye on her, too, and could concentrate on whoever else is lurking nearby.* Lee seemed genuine, but she was good at deception or she would not have been able to hide her identity for so long among people who knew her.

For long, agonizing moments they stood absolutely still. They heard only one more faint, sob-like sound, and then all was quiet—deathly so. A scrabbling sound almost under their feet brought a shriek from Lee—quickly stifled by Elliott's hand over her mouth. His own heart almost stopped beating and his mouth went dry.

He flashed on the light and they saw a grey rat. For a few seconds its tiny, beady eyes glowed red and startled in the flashlight beam, then it scurried away.

"We might as well go on to the light and see what's there," Elliott whispered.

"I'm sure it's Steven," Lee said, with a tremor in her voice. "And when I get my arms about him, I will never let anyone take me away from him again!"

"Go easy or you'll frighten the child," Elliott warned. "Remember, Steven knows Marvin but he doesn't know you as Lee Barfield. And what he has heard about his mother has undoubtedly been bad."

"I–I'll try," Lee said unsteadily.

With the flashlights still on, they moved forward. Lee tucked her frigidly cold hand into Elliott's large warm one. He felt it trembling in his grasp and squeezed it reassuringly.

They hugged the cold, rocky wall as they eased around the corner. Nothing moved as they slowly came out into another, rather narrow room. At the far end of the room, a naked light bulb glowed weakly.

A quick glance revealed that a wall of strong iron bars had been erected across the end of the narrow room. A heavy door, also made of vertical iron bars, was inset in the others.

With a small cry, Lee broke away from Elliott and ran forward to peer through the bars. In a few quick strides, Elliott stood beside her.

Laying at the back of the tiny cell was a pile of old burlap sacks. A heavy overcoat was drawn up almost to the white face of a child. As they stared in, the form stirred slightly and a soft, sobbing moan came to their ears.

Elliott felt a surge of joy rise up inside him like a mushrooming fountain, sending showers of its droplets surging along his veins. They had found Steven!

Lee was fumbling with a large padlock on the door, he suddenly realized. He bounced the beam of his flashlight back down the narrow room behind them and then into the tiny, poorly lighted room behind the barred wall and door. They were still alone, he saw with relief.

The single bulb hanging from the ceiling of the small cell cast only a little light out into the tunnel where they were standing, so Elliott used the beam of his flashlight to examine the rough rock walls for a possible key to the lock.

A quiet exclamation of delight burst from his tense lips. On a nail, driven into a seam of the rock wall back from the door hung a key!

Before Elliott could move to get the key, Lee pounced on it and with fumbling, anxious fingers inserted it into the padlock and turned it. The padlock swung down and Lee hastily removed it. As she pulled open the door, Elliott again swept the area behind them with the beam of his flashlight.

"This is too easy," Elliott muttered. His mouth felt like a Sahara wind had sandblasted it, and he could feel sweat trickling down between his shoulder blades. His heart was pounding like he had been running uphill. Everything was silent as the proverbial tomb—the analogy gave him a shiver.

The door opened with a squeal. Casting one more look outside, Elliott followed Lee inside.

"Easy," Elliott cautioned Lee as she started forward. "Let me go first. He'll know me."

"Okay," Lee said, drawing back reluctantly.

Elliott took three strides across the little room and knelt beside the small form. Laying his flashlight so it illuminated his face, he spoke softly, "Steven, wake up. It's Uncle Elliott."

The slight figure stirred, lay still a second, then catapulted upright to fling his arms around Elliott's neck in a strangling, frantic grip. Violent sobs erupted from the child's lips. "Uncle Elliott, Uncle Elliott," he said brokenly, over and over. Elliott felt hot tears on his neck.

Elliott tasted salt on his lips and realized he, too, was crying. Intense, overwhelming feelings of relief, love, and a fierce protectiveness ran through him. His heart literally ached with the joy that filled his body in a warm glow.

Suddenly, Elliott felt Steven stiffen. The child's head came up from his shoulder, and his grip about Elliott's neck tightened. Elliott swung around warily.

Lee was kneeling very close to them, her heart in her eyes. Even the weak, bare bulb hanging from the ceiling clearly illuminated the smile trembling on her pale lips. She was wiping at tears that kept overflowing her eyes.

"Who—who are you? Do I know you?" Steven asked in a puzzled voice.

"Does she look like Marvin?" asked Elliott.

"A little, but Marvin has a beard and blue eyes. Is this lady Marvin's sister?"

"No...she isn't Marvin's sister," Elliott answered slowly. "This *is* Marvin! You see, Marvin wasn't really a man; he's a woman."

"Marvin's a woman?"

"Yes, Steven, Marvin's really a woman. And a very special lady, I might add....Steven, this is your mother."

Elliott's eyes checked Lee's movement toward her son. Steven's eyes had widened with alarm, then fear glimmered in the tear-wet, grey eyes. "But–but my mother is wicked! Grandfather told me so! She k–killed my father!"

Lee spoke for the first time, and her voice was the soft husky voice of Lee Barfield. "Steven, your grandfather is mistaken. I did not kill your father."

For a moment Steven stared at Lee, then he buried his head in Elliott's shoulder, "I'm afraid of her. Please don't let her hurt me," his voice trembled into Elliott's ear, but carried plainly to Lee.

Over his small nephew's head, Elliott saw the anguish that leaped into Lee's expressive gold eyes. Her face twisted with agonizing pain.

"It's okay, Steven," Elliott soothed, "your mother would

never harm you." Even as he said the words, he hoped fervently that they were true. Although he found himself longing to do so, his common sense would not allow him to trust Lee completely.

"Steven," Lee suddenly used the deeper Marvin Maxell voice that the child knew. "Do you recognize my voice now?"

A quiver ran through Steven's small body, and his answer was muffled by the curve of Elliott's shoulder. "Yes—but you can't be Marvin. He had dark blue eyes."

"Steven, I ran away from prison because I wanted to prove to everyone that I did not murder your father. And—I wanted to be near my little boy. The reason I put on a beard and used colored contact lenses to make my eyes blue was so no one would know me and I could stay at Coppercrest."

Steven lifted his head and stared at Lee. Obviously, his curiosity was beginning to overcome his fear. "But you can't be Marvin. Girls don't know how to fix cars. Marvin changed the tire when it went flat and even made the car run real smooth when it wouldn't hardly run. I saw him!" His voice had grown somewhat scornful.

Suddenly Lee laughed. Elliott felt his heart bound. He remembered this heart-strumming, bell-like, carefree laugh of Lee's. It had been her most attractive quality. This was the first time he had heard her laugh since he returned.

"Girls can learn anything boys can, my dear little chauvinistic son," Lee said lightly. "I learned how to take a car engine apart and put it back together again in prison, and I learned to do all the things needed to keep a car running properly. I knew I would need to earn a living. I sure couldn't get my own money if I escaped. Besides—I like cars!"

"I do, too!" Steven said eagerly. "When I get big, I want to be a race car driver. Marvin..." Steven suddenly looked confused, "uh—uh, y–you said I could be anything I wanted to—if I worked hard at it. Remember?" he finished anxiously.

"I remember! And you can, too."

"You really are Marvin?" Steven said, still a little doubtful.

"I *was* Marvin, but from now on I want to be Lee Barfield—your mother," Lee said in her Marvin voice. "That is, if you will let me," she finished in her soft, husky, distinctive Lee Barfield voice.

For a long, poignant moment Steven studied Lee's face. Then he sighed. "I'm going to have to get used to you first."

Elliott saw the tenseness easing out of Lee's face as she said easily, "That's fine with me. But I want to ask you one thing. Do you think Marvin would ever have hurt you in any way?"

"Of course not!" Steven quickly replied.

"Then, just remember that I'm still the same person, but without a beard, blue eyes, and the deeper male voice. I would never, never hurt you in any way, either!"

"Okay," Steven said readily. He laid his head back on Elliott's shoulder. "But right now, I want Uncle Elliott to get me out of this awful old place."

"Who brought you here, Steven?" Elliott asked gently.

"I did!" a male voice said from the doorway. Three pairs of startled eyes swung around. Framed in the doorway was an athletic-looking, blond young man. His sun-darkened face would have been good-looking if it hadn't been wearing a triumphant sneer. His slender hands held a sawed-off shotgun.

Elliott felt shock kick him in the pit of his stomach as he looked beyond the blond young man and saw a woman there, also with a gun in her slim, shapely hand. It was Allyssa Star!

27

Elliott stared at Allyssa incredulously. She met his stare with amused, mocking eyes. Finally, he spoke in a dazed voice. "What's going on here, Allyssa?"

Before she could answer, Lee interposed in a cold, hard voice, "She kidnapped Steven, that's what!"

"But—but how could you, Allyssa?" Elliott stammered, "You're Steven's nanny, hired to take care of him."

"For money," Allyssa said easily. "You Barfields have lots of it, but my twin brother, Adam, and I have always had to scratch for enough to stay alive. Old Cyrus Barfield has plenty, so we decided he would want to share some of it with us." Her lovely voice, always so warm and soft, was derisive and harsh, her eyes, hard, cold, blue-grey granite.

"I doubt that my stepfather would pay a copper penny of ransom for me—but you could probably get a bundle for little Steven," Elliott said caustically.

Allyssa's brother chortled unpleasantly and Allyssa smiled mockingly. "What makes you think we plan to ransom any of you?" Adam said in a rasping voice.

Elliott felt a chill start at the base of his skull and travel quickly across every nerve ending.

"Can we go home now, Allyssa?" Steven interrupted. "You said I could go home when Marvin came."

"No, you little spoiled brat, you can't go home! Now, or ever!" Allyssa spat hatefully.

Steven's lips trembled and tears threatened. "Why—why are

you mad at me? Did I do something wrong?"

Elliott hugged the child protectively to his chest. "No, kid, you didn't do anything wrong. Don't worry, your Uncle Elliott will see that you get home."

Allyssa crowded past Adam and glared belligerently at Elliott. "The big tough news-guy will take care of you, Steven dear," she said sarcastically.

She drew her diminutive figure up to her full five feet, two inches and laughed. "The truth of it, Elliott, is that I hadn't planned for you to be here. If Steven's jailbird mother hadn't brought you, you could still be in your cozy bed at Coppercrest!"

"You were the one who set me free?" Lee interjected.

"Sure! And I also set it up for you to escape from prison. Aren't I the nice one?" Allyssa's laugh dripped with poison.

"And you are the two I heard talking in the parking lot of the Gypsy Blue buildings, the night of Steven's abduction?" Elliott said slowly.

"And you nearly caught us!"

Lee stood up and took a step forward.

"Keep your distance, lady," Adam warned.

Ignoring him, Lee stopped where she was and asked softly, "Why did you need me out of prison and jail? So I would be available to have a new murder pinned on me?"

"This dame isn't so dumb," Adam chortled.

Allyssa's face twisted with hatred as she stared at Lee. "So you want to know what I need with you? Well, let me tell you a few things that may shock your socks off. You almost lost your handsome husband to me a few years ago."

She lifted the polished, turquoise nugget that again hung about her neck on a delicate silver chain. "See this necklace? Your adorable husband gave it to me."

"So you lied to me about that, too," Elliott said bitterly. "Austin gave you his venomous trophy!"

Allyssa ignored his remark and pierced Lee with eyes that

were darkened with rage, "Austin was going to divorce you and marry me! Then he chickened out—because you tried to convince him your marriage might be salvaged. Those were his very words!"

Lee's face was white as paper. "So Austin *was* seeing someone else," she choked. "And he swore he wasn't!"

"Sure he was seeing my sister, had been for months," Adam said cruelly. "It was Allyssa's and my plan for her to become Austin's wife so she would have lots of money. Then she was going to share it with me."

"So you two killed Austin," Lee said through tight lips.

"I did!" Allyssa said maliciously. "I was supposed to meet him at the bottom of the stone stairway that runs up from the street to Coppercrest. When he was late, I walked up the stairs. I had heard voices arguing and when I got close, I saw you and Austin in that little garden, having a bang-up quarrel.

"Austin told you he wouldn't allow you to go away even for a temporary separation, so I realized he was lying to me and didn't plan to divorce you at all! That arrogant liar was just playing me for a fool!"

"So you sneaked up behind him and fractured his skull with the pipe wrench Lee had thrown down," Elliott said.

"Right!" Allyssa said triumphantly. "And he deserved it! That was the last time he played *me* for a fool. When I heard Lee threaten him with a wrench when he hit her, I thought she was going to have the gumption to kill him herself."

"I could never have killed anyone," Lee said with a shudder, "especially my husband. I loved him...in spite of everything."

"You were a stupid fool," Allyssa hissed. "When I saw you throw the wrench down and run upstairs, I crept up the steps and onto the grass behind him and picked up the wrench. I used a scarf I was wearing so my fingerprints wouldn't be on the wrench. Austin was too busy laughing at you to notice me!"

Elliott glanced at Steven and saw the child's eyes, wide and horror-filled, almost hypnotically glued to Allyssa's face.

Elliott longed to stop the child's ears from hearing the grisly details but knew it was probably for the best. At least Steven would never again believe his mother had killed his father.

Allyssa was gloating with her sordid story. "As soon as you entered the house, Lee, I let him have it. He fell like a downed ox! Never even whimpered once!"

For a moment, Elliott wondered if Lee was going to faint. She swayed, took a couple of steps backward and leaned against the wall with closed eyes.

"What a ninny you are," Allyssa said fiercely. "That man beat you and scorned you and yet you still cared for him! He would never have dared treat me that way!"

Lee drew in a ragged breath and straightened up. "Love is a strange thing. Sometimes it takes a lot to kill it," she said. "And in spite of everything Austin did, he was still a human being. No matter how he wronged you…or me…he didn't deserve to die like that."

"You said you hadn't planned for me to be here with Lee and Steven," Elliott interposed, his voice bitter, "I suppose you had other plans for me!"

"She was going to marry *you*," Adam said bluntly.

A flush rose in Allyssa's cheeks, and she slapped her brother's arm sharply, "You don't have to tell everything you know!"

"So I was going to take Austin's place—after you found out I was a fourth owner of Gypsy Blue Enterprises!"

Allyssa dropped her eyes, but only for a few seconds, then she lifted her head proudly and said scathingly, " One has to take advantage of situations as they present themselves."

"I guess becoming Steven's nanny was also part of your plan?" Lee asked. "So you could get your claws in Gentry and marry him." Although her face was still pale, Lee's voice had hardened.

"Of course! Austin had already introduced him to me at a party once!"

"And how could the queenly siren condescend to marry

Gentry?" Elliott asked tauntingly. "He is only the business manager for Gypsy Blue!"

"He's also the illegitimate son of Cyrus—and Tilda," Allyssa shot back. "I'll bet you didn't know that!"

Elliott was so staggered by this piece of news that he could only stand and gape. "I don't believe it!" he finally said.

"It's true, nevertheless," Allyssa said triumphantly. "Tilda told me when Gentry and I started dating, shortly after I came here. She had a paper to prove it. Tilda told me bitterly that Cyrus Barfield felt it was beneath him to marry his housekeeper, but he did promise—in writing—to educate Gentry and give him a good job when he was grown."

Her voice went coy. "Tilda saw that her son was smitten with me, and she told me that Gentry was Cyrus's son so I'd know what a good catch he was!"

"Does Gentry know?" Elliott asked.

"No, but Tilda had felt for a long time that Cyrus might give Gentry some shares in the business. So when Mr. Barfield refused to even make her son the guardian for Steven, she began to worry that he'd never do more for him than he has now. She has been considering telling Gentry so he could press his rights as an heir of the old man, if he so desired."

"So you hoped to be the wife of one of the heirs of Gypsy Blue—and it didn't really matter which," Lee interjected.

Allyssa laughed unpleasantly. "Well, I would have preferred to be the wife of Austin or Elliott—the prestige and all—but I still plan to be the wife of a Barfield and his fortune! I plan to be Gentry's wife! He adores me! And we will press his claim as an heir, I can tell you with certainty!"

And to think I was interested in that beautiful doll with a heart of ice, Elliott thought. Hot anger burned in his chest until a sudden, chilling thought cooled it: This was no time for regret or anger. Allyssa and her brother did not plan for them to leave the mine alive!

28

"What are you going to do with us?" Elliott asked, rising to his feet, spilling Steven gently to the ground. The child clung to his legs.

"Sit back down!" ordered Adam.

"My legs have gone to sleep," Elliott said. "I need to stretch them. It won't take a minute."

When Adam did not order him to sit down again, Elliott unlocked Steven's arms and looked down into the child's uplifted, frightened face. "Let me get the kinks out of my legs, little buddy," he said gently.

He took a couple of stiff steps and leaned against the side wall of the small room, lifting and flexing each leg gingerly.

Elliott was thinking fast. He had purposely moved away from Steven and Lee. But the small room did not allow him to put much space between them.

That Allyssa and Adam planned to murder all three of them was a certainty in his mind. He grew objective and calm, wondering if he could get his gun out and shoot both of them before they killed him.

But Allyssa's sarcastic voice cut into his racing thoughts. "Don't try to be a hero, Elliott. Adam and I will cut you down before you can make a move of any kind. Turn around slowly with your hands against the wall and your feet apart."

With a sinking heart, Elliott did as he was told.

"Adam, he probably has a weapon. I'll cover him; you search him." Her voice was as cold as a glacial wind.

Within seconds, Adam had found and taken Elliott's gun and pocketknife. Then, with Adam gleefully holding his shotgun on Elliott, Allyssa searched Lee. She found nothing.

"Okay, sit back down! Both of you!" Allyssa ordered. "Elliott, sit here close to Lee so Adam will hit you both if he has to use his shotgun!"

Steven had been cowering on the floor, but as soon as Elliott and Lee were again seated, he huddled between them and clung to Elliott's arm.

Lee lifted her head and said quickly, "Allyssa, Mr. Barfield would pay a fortune in ransom for Steven. You could hold us until the money is delivered and then go to Mexico—or some other country—and live like kings. But if you kill us, the law will hound you until it catches you."

"Ha!" Allyssa hooted. "No one will ever know that we did it! Who's to tell? Besides, I've already killed Austin, so if I *was* caught, I could only be electrocuted once—whether I killed one or four!"

"Things have a way of catching up with you, Allyssa," Elliott said. "Perhaps you don't have anything to lose but Adam does. He isn't a murderer—yet."

He turned to Adam, who was watching him through narrowed, thoughtful eyes. "Adam, you could both get plenty of money by ransoming us, with lots less risk. What do you say?"

"I say *no*," Allyssa said hotly.

Adam was silent for a moment while he stared at Elliott. Then he said slowly, "He's right, Allyssa. I haven't killed anybody yet. I put that car out of gear and gave it a shove down the street in Bisbee, but Steven got out of the way so quick it didn't hurt him. And I tampered with the latch on that gate and pushed the lawn mower down the stairway. But no one was killed. Maybe we should just get a million or two in ransom and skip the country."

"Don't be stupid!" Allyssa yelled furiously. "If we don't get rid of all three of them, there will be witnesses who can put the law after us."

Her voice suddenly softened, and she laid a hand on Adam's arm. "Adam, we must do it like we planned. It is the only way. Can't you see? With them gone, we'll be free. But if we take a ransom and run, we'll always be running."

"But I don't like the idea of killing three people."

"Neither do I, Adam," Allyssa said softly, "but it's the only thing we can do now."

Adam hesitated, then agreed reluctantly. "I suppose so."

Allyssa's eyes glinted, "Think about all the money we'll have when I'm married to Gentry. Old man Barfield will be glad to make Gentry his heir when he has no one else to inherit and run his precious Gypsy Blue Enterprises! When he's dead—and anyone can see he's on his last leg—I'll be Gentry's wife and we'll live like we've always wanted to."

The gleam in Allyssa's eyes was reflected in Adam's. "Sure! And maybe after a while, Gentry will have an accident. Then we will own it all!"

"You have it all planned," Elliott said bitingly, "but how will you account to God with the blood of all of us on your heads? Just so you can inherit this Deadly Gypsy Blue?"

For a second both Allyssa and Adam looked startled, and then Allyssa threw back her head and laughed. "So—in his last hours, the strong newspaper guy thinks of God!"

"Perhaps you should think about Him, too," Lee interposed quietly. "There is a Scripture that says, 'He who lives by the sword will die by the sword.'"

"We aren't going to kill you with a sword; we're much more modern than that," Allyssa taunted. "We're going to use a bomb to send you to the other world." She waved her hand toward the tunnel. "It's just over there, so I would advise you to start saying your prayers—you'll be meeting your Maker soon!"

"Allyssa," Lee's voice was trembling, "you have taken care of Steven! Tucked him in at night! Read stories to him!" Her voice had dropped to a whisper of anguish, "Please—doesn't that mean something to you?"

"Not a thing!" Allyssa said coldly. "I hated every moment of taking care of him. The spoiled little rich boy! Heir to all the Gypsy Blue wealth. And I got peanuts for putting up with him. Besides, he's the son of the man who used me! I hope Austin knows I'm sending his son to heaven on a fast express!"

"Let's cut the conversation and get out of here," Adam interrupted suddenly.

"Why, Adam, I do believe all this stuff about God and heaven and death is getting to you." Allyssa laughed lightly. "Are you forgetting that to get anywhere in this life, we have to be tough? Tough, Adam! And that's what we are. Remember?"

"It might get you possessions in this life, Adam," Elliott said softly, "but this life is very short, seventy years—maybe a few more if God allows them—and then what? Eternity is a long, *long* time. Especially if you are in the wrong place."

Allyssa's eyes narrowed as fear flickered over her brother's face. Abruptly, she leaped across the small cell and struck Elliott across the cheek with the barrel of her gun.

Elliott reeled under the impact of the blow and brilliant lights seemed to be flashing behind his eyes while agonizing pain seared his cheekbone. He tried to shake the blindness from his eyes, but his head seemed gripped in a red haze of pain.

"You coward!" Lee said furiously, scrambling to her knees.

Allyssa quickly backed away from them, and said menacingly, "I wouldn't try anything heroic, Mrs. *Austin* Barfield! Unless you want a dose of the same medicine!"

Steven put his small arm around Elliott's shoulders and said heatedly to Allyssa. "You are wicked and—and mean! Let my Uncle Elliott—and my—my mother alone!"

Lee put out her hand, and Steven took it with his free right hand, pressing it to his chest.

"Let's leave this little family scene before I lose my dinner," Allyssa said scoffingly. She edged past her brother and stepped back into the shaft. Adam backed out, too, and both stood looking into the cell for a moment.

"You have about an hour," Allyssa said. "Then enough dynamite to bring the roof down will cover this room and you all forever. In fact, it should cave-in this whole worked-out section. You've got an hour to get acquainted with your tomb. I doubt that your bodies will ever be found!"

"And I thought you were so sweet and gentle," Elliott muttered caustically.

He could focus his eyes again but his cheekbone felt like it had been cracked open. He put up a hand and felt his face. To his amazement, his probing fingers found only a small cut. It hurt like it had been sliced to the bone! He felt blood oozing from it.

Allyssa chuckled maliciously. "We're all wrong once in a while. Adam and I will be back in our beds long before the bomb goes off," she jeered. "I'll leave some evidence outside that will prove the loony Lee Barfield broke out of jail and blew up part of the Gypsy Blue Mine, herself, her son—and the other heir to Deadly Gypsy Blue, as our dear Elliott is so fond of calling his stepfather's lucrative business."

Elliott jumped to his feet as Adam swung the iron door closed with a crash and quickly snapped the padlock closed.

"Good-bye, all!" Allyssa's taunting words floated back to them as she and her brother started away. "We'll take the key—just to be sure you don't leave the party too soon." Allyssa's and Adam's mocking laughter trailed away. The three in the cell heard the brief crunch of retreating footsteps on the rocky floor and steps going down the wooden ladder. Then silence settled around them.

Elliott, Lee, and Steven dashed to the bars. Pale light from the single light bulb dimly illuminated the walls beyond the iron bars. Lee's face was ashen as she turned to Elliott. "What are we going to do?"

29

"I don't know," Elliott said slowly, "but we have an hour before that bomb goes off. Let's see if we can find a way out of here."

Lee stared out into the tunnel at the small red light glowing implacably just ten feet away. "They had it all set up and ready for us," she said angrily.

"And as they were leaving, they activated it," Elliott said.

He drew in a deep breath and exhaled slowly to calm the fear that was hammering in his chest and knotting his stomach.

Lee suddenly leaned over and touched a gentle finger to Elliott's cheek. "Does it hurt terribly?"

"It's getting better," Elliott said, even though it throbbed like a toothache. "We've a lot worse things to think of right now than a bruised cheek."

"A–are we going to d–die?" Steven asked.

"Not if we can help it!" Elliott replied grimly.

He went to the vertical bars and examined both ends closely where they were attached to the rocky wall. Time and care had been expended on setting the heavy metal bars into the wall, he saw. Adam—or whoever had engineered the project—had known what he was doing. The iron-bar wall and door were constructed so well that even Elliott's most violent jerking and pulling scarcely shook them.

Lee, with Steven now standing close to her, his hand in hers, watched Elliott's efforts silently. She said doubtfully, "Could we dig under the wall?"

"It's worth a try, if we can find anything to dig with," Elliott said, picking up his flashlight and swinging it around the small prison. "What's this?" he exclaimed, noticing a curtain across the corner of the room for the first time.

"It's the bathroom," Steven said, darting across to pull open the curtain. A small chemical toilet, a two-gallon thermos and a small plastic wash pan rested on the rough rock floor.

"Adam brought me water in that every day," he said, pointing to the thermos. "I had to drink out of the lid."

"Did he bring you food, too?" Lee asked.

"Yes—mostly hamburgers and fries. They were always cold, but they tasted good anyway when I got real hungry."

Lee knelt down and looked into Steven's face, "Why did your piano teacher let you go with Adam? Surely you told her he wasn't the chauffeur!"

Steven's lips trembled. "He–he had on a beard and l–looked like Marvin. I didn't think his voice sounded r–right but he hurried me off so fast, I didn't have time to think about it. He told the teacher that Miss Star was really sick and had to go home right away."

"And then he brought you here?"

"Yes. At first I was excited that Marvin was bringing me to see the mine again. I like the Gypsy Blue Mine. I asked him if we were going to get Allyssa first and take her home but he wouldn't answer me. Then I began to get scared. When I looked closer, he didn't really look like Marvin, after all! Then when we got here, he took off the beard and wig and said I was to call him Adam."

"Did he hurt you in any way?" asked Elliott.

"No–o. But before we got to the mine, I was so scared I started to cry, and he told me to shut up or he would give me something to cry about!

"Adam yelled at me when I didn't stop, then he shut me in and slammed the door and went out and left me in the dark. He said he would turn the light on when I quit crying. I tried to stop, but for a while, I couldn't."

"Did he leave you in the dark for very long?" Elliott asked, anger thick in his voice.

"For a long time," Steven said with a quavering voice. "I called and called and, finally, he came back and turned the light on. He said if I wouldn't cry, he would always leave me a light, but if I cried, he would turn it off. So I didn't cry anymore." He hesitated, "Well, not so he could hear me, anyway."

"I'm so proud of you," Lee said softly. "You were a very brave boy."

As they were talking, Elliott had been yanking and pulling at the curtain. Suddenly, the rod broke into two pieces. He twisted and jerked until one piece came free of the wall. Then he twisted the other piece until it also came loose.

"These aren't very good digging tools, but they seem to be the best we have," Elliott said. "And we can use the cap of the thermos to scoop out the dirt."

Lee nodded and quickly picked up one of the bent curtain rods. Taking her flashlight, she examined the floor along the bottom of the iron wall. "This ground looks like rock. I don't think any place looks softer than another, do you?"

"I'm afraid not." Elliott began to scratch at the ground along the bottom of the wall with the other half of the curtain rod.

They dug laboriously for several minutes, scraping out pitifully small quantities of dirt with the thermos lid.

"There must be a rock there now," Lee said suddenly. "I can't dig out any more dirt."

They turned their flashlight beams into the small indentation in the earth, and Elliott suddenly sat back with an angry exclamation, "Concrete! They set the iron bars in a ledge of concrete!"

"Can't we tunnel under it, too?" Lee asked.

"We can try," Elliott said, "but as hard and rocky as the ground is, it looks pretty hopeless."

After a few more minutes of exhausting work, Lee laid her

curtain rod down and rose to her feet. "There's solid rock under the concrete," she said dispiritedly.

Elliott rose and brushed his sweat-damp hair back with a dirt-stained hand, leaving a dark streak on his high forehead. "It's hopeless, I'm afraid," he agreed wearily. "We've been digging for thirty minutes and this hole isn't deep enough for a mouse to hide in. Obviously, this room has been made as foolproof as they could make it."

He stared through the bars and ground his teeth together savagely. Past the pale yellow light, in the darkness, the red eye of the bomb glowed mockingly.

Steven's voice suddenly broke the silence, "Uncle Elliott." It fell thin and high with fright on Elliott's tortured soul. Looking from one to the other, Steven asked, "C–can't we g–get out before the bomb goes off?"

Elliott dropped down on one knee, pulled Steven into his arms, and held him close to his chest. He said nothing. His helplessness was maddening. The child burrowed his head into Elliott's shoulder for a moment and then lifted beseeching eyes to Elliott. "We—we are going to die, aren't we?"

Lee sank down and looked into Steven's face, "Steven, you aren't a very big boy, but I won't lie to you. We may be going to die."

Elliott made an inarticulate sound of protest, but Lee went on firmly, "Remember, you gave your heart to Jesus a few weeks ago at church. He has a wonderful place for His children ready in heaven. If you die, you will just go to live in heaven with Jesus."

Steven's eyes were wide and solemn upon Lee's face, "How—how do you know?"

"Because the Bible says so," Lee said gently but adamantly. "And the Bible and God do not lie!"

"And—and heaven is a nice place?"

"A very wonderful place! There are no bad people there to hurt others. No one in heaven is ever sick, and no one is ever sad.

Your grandma is there and Jesus himself will be there with you, and you will never be afraid of anything again."

A lump the size of an orange swelled up in Elliott's throat. He no longer doubted that Lee knew the Lord. Her simple words of faith felt like warm oil running through his troubled spirit.

Steven reached up to put his small arm around Elliott's neck and laid his smooth, silky cheek against Elliott's face. His voice was still solemn as he addressed Lee, "Will you and Uncle Elliott be there with me?"

Lee's face swam before Elliott's eyes as a mist rose in his eyes, but he heard her answer with vivid clarity. "I will be, little son, and I hope your Uncle Elliott will be there, too."

Steven slowly disengaged himself from Elliott's arms and drew back to look up into his face. He put a small forefinger to Elliott's face and said wonderingly, "You're crying, Uncle Elliott. Does your cheek hurt—or are you sad because we're going to die and go to heaven to be with Jesus?"

Elliott had not known till then that he was crying. Self-consciously, he rubbed at his eyes with a grubby fist. He winced as his hand touched his bruised cheek.

Looking directly into Steven's eyes, he said gently, "I also have given my life to Jesus, little buddy—a few days ago."

He heard Lee's softly indrawn breath and turned toward her. Her face came into focus and he saw that her eyes were also wet. An oddly bewildering thought flashed into his mind: *Lee is a lovely woman!*

Her gold eyes, speckled with darker, greenish-copper flecks, seemed to glow in her thin, delicately formed, triangular face. It was strange that this woman had ever successfully hidden her very feminine face—even behind a beard!

"I'm so glad," she said softly. "Now we are all three ready to meet God, if He doesn't grant us a miracle and get us out of here."

"But we can pray for that miracle," Elliott said firmly. "Lee, would you begin?"

Lee hesitated for a moment, then reached over to take Elliott's and Steven's hands in her cool, slim ones. She bowed her head and began to pray, almost inaudibly at first and then stronger and more confidently.

"Father, I know I have failed you miserably. Please forgive me for the lies I've told, and the lie I have lived at Coppercrest the past weeks. Forgive me for not trusting you and for setting about to work things out myself instead of trusting you to take care of Steven and me. Perhaps if I had trusted you as I should, none of us would be entombed here.

"You know our desperate situation. We ask you to deliver us from this prison. We know you can—but if you choose not to do so, give us courage and peace to accept what comes to us. In Jesus' name we pray. Amen."

Elliott was amazed at the calmness and peace stealing over him. A comforting but awesome presence seemed to fill the little room, and he heard himself praying, "Thank you, Father, for forgiving my sins and making me clean and fit for heaven. Thank you for your peace that fills my heart. Thank you for giving me life. I trust you now as we face death. Amen."

He thought in wonder, *So this is why Mother could still love the Lord, even when she didn't understand why things happened!*

Suddenly, Elliott reached out and pulled both Steven and Lee into his arms, and they did not resist. Steven laid his head on one shoulder and Lee laid her face against his other.

The moments ticked away and Elliott wondered how much time they had left but he didn't look at his watch. Beyond the bars, he could see the steady glow of the red eye of the bomb. For a moment, panic and fear threatened to engulf him. Then that inexplicable peace again settled upon him and he whispered softly, "We're ready now, Lord. We are in your hands!"

30

The minutes ticked slowly away. *How long ago it seems since I was on my last news assignment,* Elliott thought. *And after all the dangerous assignments I have covered and survived, here I'm going to die in a mine under a mountain in Bisbee, Arizona. In my childhood hometown. How ironic.*

Lee stirred in his arms and sat up. "I hear something," she said. "Listen!"

Steven abruptly sat up and said excitedly, "I hear voices!"

A few seconds later, Elliott also heard distant sounds: voices, hurried footsteps, and the clink of a metal object against rock. The sounds grew louder and, suddenly, light filled the room around the corner.

The three of them ran to the barred wall and waited in silence.

Elliott could hear heavy footsteps and his heart quickened. The steps sounded too heavy for either Allyssa or her brother. And there was too much light for only two flashlights.

A shout carried around the corner to them, "Elliott, Lee, are you there?"

A slight chill tickled Elliott's backbone. It was Gentry's voice! Was he enemy or friend? Gentry had a lot to gain if all three of them were dead! Was he part of it?

But Steven had no such thoughts. When neither Elliott nor Lee answered, he called loudly, "Gentry—we're here, locked in! There's a bomb out there that's going to go off!"

Gentry came puffing into view in the thin light that streamed weakly from their light bulb. He was dripping wet with sweat as if he had been running all the way. "I–I know there's a bomb," he panted. In his hands he held a pair of bolt cutters. "We'll have you out of there pronto," he gasped, sliding to a stop in front of the iron bars.

"Gentry," Steven said excitedly, "Marvin wasn't a man. He's my mother! And my mother didn't kill my father. Allyssa did!"

"I know," Gentry said grimly, "and she almost got away with it." He was working frantically with the bolt cutters.

Another voice spoke, brisk and commanding from farther down the tunnel. "Get them out of there quick, Gentry, and we'll see if I can disarm this bomb before it goes off!"

Now Elliott could make out the figures of Police Chief Richter and a husky young deputy near the steady red glow of the bomb light. They were being rescued! He had reconciled himself to death and the thought of life left him almost dizzy with relief.

As soon as Gentry had the padlock off, Lee grabbed Steven's hand and darted through the door. Elliott hesitated.

"Come on," Gentry urged. "Let's get out of here. That bomb couldn't have much time left on it."

"It's got five minutes," Chief Richter shouted. "Get out of here! Now!"

"Go on with Gentry," Elliott said to Lee. "I'll be right behind you." He strode quickly to where the deputy was holding a bright light for Chief Richter. "Don't try to disarm that bomb," he urged quickly. "The risk is too great. Come on with us—let it blow!"

"Get out of here," the chief said forcefully. "I've had training and experience with bombs, and this looks like a simple one. But if I can't disarm it, we'll make a run for it—and we don't want you in our way. Go! Go!"

Elliott took off at a run. Gentry, Lee and Steven were already down the first ladder and almost to the second, he saw by their bobbing lights.

"Thank you, Father, for saving our lives," he said humbly as he ran.

He had never before experienced the keen exhilaration that suffused him. *We're alive!* he thought as he scrambled down the first ladder and ran toward the second.

He caught up with Gentry, Lee, and Steven as they turned into the last tunnel. Gentry and Lee had Steven between them and were fairly flying, lifting Steven off the ground as they ran. He was laughing with delight.

Jogging up beside Lee, Elliott suggested he take Steven's hand and she relinquished it. As Gentry and Elliott swung Steven along, Lee raced behind them. They burst from the mine entrance into the early morning darkness and stopped.

Lee crouched down and put her arms around Steven. For a moment he gazed at her under the glow of the mercury lights, then, seeming to have decided something in his mind, he snuggled into her arms. Her wet eyes met Elliott's over his small brown head. A tremulous smile curved her lips and she laughed softly.

A quiver ran through Elliott as he met her eyes. Then he walked back to the entrance where Gentry stood looking into the opening. Gentry turned toward Elliott, concern vivid on his strong features.

"Do you think they'll make it?" Elliott asked.

"Chief Richter will pull it off, if anyone can," Gentry said.

Suddenly from down in the shaft came the hollow sound of voices and the crunch of footsteps. Both Gentry and Elliott sighed with relief.

Elliott turned to Gentry. "How did you know we were down in the mine?"

Gentry smiled his rare grin. "I did a bit of detective work," he said. "I haven't been able to sleep well since Steven disappeared, so when I couldn't sleep, I went down to the family room. I was putting a video tape in the VCR when I heard a slight sound in the hall. I went to investigate and saw Allyssa slipping out of the house."

He paused and Elliott saw pain in his eyes.

"For some reason, I had never felt Allyssa's story about Steven's disappearance was very plausible, so I followed her. I was sure glad later that I keep a camcorder in my car...and that I followed her."

"That was pretty dangerous," Elliott said. "She and her brother both had guns."

"I didn't know at first that he was her brother," Gentry said. "She picked him up at the Oliver House—a small inn downtown. I didn't know until we got to the mine that they had guns.

"Anyway, I drove without headlights in the moonlight and was able to keep their car lights in sight. I left my car a little ways down the road from the mine when I realized they were coming here. I grabbed my camcorder and sneaked up to the parking lot; I could see them quite well under the mercury lights. I saw him take what looked like a sawed-off shotgun out of a case. And Allyssa stuck a handgun in her belt. I was sure wishing I had thought of taking a weapon then!"

"Did you follow them down into the mine, or wait up here for them to come out?"

"I gave them a couple of minutes to get down the tunnel, and then I followed them in," Gentry said. "I used their light to guide me." He chuckled grimly. "I fell once when my foot slipped on a loose piece of ore. It's a good thing I know this place better than the palm of my hand. It's as dark as the inside of a whale's belly.

"And I got the movie of my life when I got up there where they were holding Steven prisoner! I saw them sneak up on you and Lee and listened to your little reunion. In fact...I got it all on the camcorder!"

"You got it all? Even after they locked us in?" Elliott asked excitedly.

"Every bit!" Gentry declared.

"Then you have the evidence to convict Allyssa of murdering Austin...and to clear Lee!"

"Yep! And of the attempted murder of all three of you!"

"How are we ever going to thank you?" Lee interjected softly from the sideline. She and Steven had moved up to listen. Steven slipped his hand into Elliott's. He looked down and squeezed it gently.

"We owe our lives to you, Gentry, there's no doubt about that," Elliott said. "And for now, all we can do is say thank you!"

Gentry looked extremely uncomfortable but pleased at the same time.

The chief and his deputy came out of the mine and Steven asked excitedly, "Did you kill the bomb?"

Chief Richter chuckled and stepped over to lay a hand on Steven's shoulder. "Dead as a doornail, young man!"

"Good," breathed the child. "I don't like loud booms. Besides, it would have blown up our Gypsy Blue Mine."

"How did you manage to get out of the mine without Allyssa or her brother seeing you?" Elliott asked Gentry.

"I almost didn't," he replied gravely. "I had gone just around the corner where I could hear and tape what was going on. I died a thousand deaths thinking they would flash their lights around and see me. But, fortunately, they felt so secure that they didn't."

"I'm anxious to see and hear the videotape," the chief said. "As soon as Gentry reached the police station, we jumped in our car and raced up here."

"How did you get away without Allyssa and Adam seeing you?" Lee asked Gentry.

"Well, I stayed as long as I dared—so I could tape as much as I could. When I saw they were about to leave, I got out of there! I sneaked back to my car and took off for town as fast as my car could go—without any lights!"

"And came directly to the police station," the chief finished.

"I thought of trying to rescue you," Gentry said, "but decided without weapons it was safer to get the chief and come back. I had heard Allyssa say the bomb wouldn't go off for an hour."

"By the way, young lady," Chief Richter said sternly to Lee, "How did you get out of my jail?"

Lee looked distressed. "Are you going to arrest me again?"

"No, but you should stick around because there will be some paper work to do. And I do want to know how you got out of my jail!"

"Allyssa arranged it," Gentry interjected. "I heard her say—and it should be on the tape—that she arranged both of Lee's escapes."

"I didn't know who helped me get out either time, but I grabbed at the chance to escape from prison so I could come here to try and find out who framed me," Lee said. "Then tonight, I knew it was probably a trap but when I was instructed to come to the mine because Steven was here, I had no choice but to come."

"I'll have to find out how she managed both escapes," the chief said grimly. "Someone at the jail and the prison must have taken bribes to help release you...and I want to catch them."

"Does Allyssa or her brother have any idea they are about to be arrested?" Lee asked.

"I don't think so, but I left orders for them both to be apprehended," the chief said. "They should be in jail by the time we get back."

31

Two hours later a weary but exuberant party arrived back at Coppercrest. The sun was just coming up. Asking the others to wait, Elliott knocked lightly at Cyrus's door.

"It's Elliott, sir," he said. "We've some good news!"

"Come on in," Cyrus called.

Elliott drew Steven into the room with him. To his surprise, he saw that Cyrus, wearing a dressing gown, was already up, sitting in his easy chair. His face was haggard and drawn, and his eyes were bloodshot as if he had not slept much.

When he saw Steven, the old man's face lit up, and he cried out hoarsely, "You found him!" He rose shakily to his feet and said eagerly, "Come over here, Stevie boy, and let me see if you're all right!"

Elliott gently nudged Steven toward his grandfather.

Steven moved forward reluctantly, but his eyes never left his grandfather's face as he advanced. When he was a step away, he stopped and looked up at Cyrus. "Are you sick, Grandfather? You—you don't look so good."

Cyrus settled back wearily into his chair. Reaching out with a slightly unsteady hand, he drew Steven to his knees. "Yes, I've been sick, child, but I'll be much better now that you've been found."

Steven looked solemnly into Cyrus's face. "Are you really glad I came back?"

"What a question!" Cyrus exclaimed. "Of course I'm glad

you came back. I've hardly slept a wink since you disappeared."

"Because if I had died you wouldn't have had anyone to run Gypsy Blue Enterprises when you're gone?"

Cyrus's keen old eyes showed surprise—and pain—to Elliott's amazement. He laid a thin hand on Steven's shoulder and spoke hesitantly. "No, Steven, not just because you are my heir...but...because I care about you."

His voice roughened and his voice dropped almost to a whisper. "I never dreamed I cared so much for you, child. I've missed you terribly and have been worried sick!"

"You won't think I was very b–brave," Steven said with suddenly lowered eyes. "I—I was scared—and I cried—when that man kidnapped me."

"Of course you were frightened!" Cyrus said. "Who wouldn't have been!"

"You aren't ashamed of me?" Steven asked, looking intently into his grandfather's face.

"Not a bit," Cyrus said stoutly. "Now, do I get a hug from my grandson?"

Steven regarded his grandfather with a solemn gaze, "If you're sure..."

"Come here, boy," Cyrus said brusquely. He leaned over and drew Steven into a fierce hug. For a moment, the child stood stiffly, then he threw his arms around his grandfather's neck and clung there.

Over the child's small head, Elliott glimpsed Cyrus's face. Down the deep furrows of his face ran a stream of real tears!

After a moment, Steven lifted his head and drew back to look into his grandfather's face. His voice was grave, "Grandfather, my mother is not a wicked woman like you said."

A cloud seemed to slide over Cyrus's face but he answered amiably enough, although with faint sarcasm, "I would call murdering one's husband very wicked." He dabbed away the wetness from his face with a large white handkerchief.

Steven stepped back away from Cyrus and stood straight and tall. "But my mother didn't kill my father. Allyssa did. And she had her brother, Adam, kidnap me and if Gentry hadn't come, she would have killed me and my mother and Uncle Elliott with a bomb in Gypsy Blue Mine!"

"Who–what is the boy saying?" Cyrus asked in bewilderment.

Before Elliott could answer, Steven ran to Elliott and pointed up to his face. "Allyssa is the wicked woman! Not Mother. Look what she did to Uncle Elliott's face! She hit him in the face with a gun!"

Cyrus rose stiffly and took a couple of steps toward Elliott and peered up at him. "You *are* hurt! D–did *Allyssa* really do that to you?"

"Yes," Elliott said a bit dryly, "our lovely little nanny is really a very deadly woman. She didn't like something I said, and she tried to break my cheekbone!"

"S–sit down and tell me all about this," Cyrus said faintly. "You say Lee didn't kill my son?" He moved back and sank into his chair again.

"No, sir, Allyssa did," Steven reiterated stoutly. "And, do you know what, Grandfather? Marvin isn't a man! He's my mother! And–and I like her—almost as much as I like Uncle Elliott," he finished almost defiantly.

"I know Marvin is really Lee and about her deceiving us all," Cyrus said tartly. He looked keenly at Steven. "And you say Allyssa killed my son and tried to kill you? I wasn't aware that she even knew Austin. Why would she want to murder him?"

"Because she wanted to marry my father and he wouldn't leave my mother," Steven said promptly. "She wanted my father's money."

"According to Allyssa, Austin had promised to divorce Lee and marry her," Elliott explained. "Then, she overheard Lee and Austin arguing in the little garden and realized—from his words—that he was only stringing her along and had no intention of leaving his wife for her."

"So Allyssa killed him!" Cyrus said faintly.

"Exactly," Elliott said. "After Lee ran up to her room, Allyssa struck him on the head with the wrench Lee had threatened him with, then vanished back down the stone stairway to the street."

"And I was so certain Lee had done it!" Cyrus said. "What an injustice has been done to that poor girl!"

"You aren't mad at Mother anymore then?" Steven asked anxiously.

"I'm not mad at anyone anymore," Cyrus said mysteriously. He looked quickly at Elliott, "Have they caught Allyssa—and this brother Steven spoke of?"

"Yes, sir," Elliott said. "They were arrested as Allyssa was dropping off her brother at the Oliver House, where he was staying."

"Steven said Gentry rescued you. Where is he? Call him in! I want to hear the whole story—every detail."

Elliott went to the door and called to Gentry and Lee.

When Cyrus saw Lee with Gentry, his keen old eyes swept her from head to toe. "So," he said gruffly, "my daughter-in-law has been impersonating a chauffeur in my house for several months."

Lee met his eyes with a slight lift to her chin, but her face was very pale.

Before she could speak, Elliott rushed to her defense. "She had no choice, sir. It was the only way that she could try to prove her innocence!"

"And she's a good chauffeur," Steven said quickly. "She can fix cars like a man!"

A gleam sparkled in Cyrus's eyes, "Ah—I see she has a couple of champions."

"I really didn't like to deceive you, sir, but when someone helped me escape, wise or not, I accepted the opportunity," Lee said defensively.

"And who helped you to escape? My sister Jessica, I suppose," Cyrus said dryly.

"No, sir," Elliott interposed. "Allyssa managed to get her out of prison."

Cyrus eyed Elliott speculatively. "Allyssa again, huh? Well, everyone sit down. I want to hear the whole story down to the last detail. I'll ring for Tilda and have her bring us all some breakfast and then we'll begin."

After the delicious breakfast Tilda prepared was consumed greedily by the weary party, and the story told, Cyrus dismissed Lee and Steven to their rooms with brusque orders to rest.

"No work today for you, either," he told Gentry. "Call the workers and tell them it's a paid holiday. My children are all home safely and no one works!"

"If you'd stay for a few moments, I have some things I wish to discuss with you, Elliott," he said. "It shouldn't take long. I know you must be very tired, too."

When the others were gone, Elliott sat back in a recliner. His cheekbone throbbed and suddenly he was extremely tired, but he had some things he wished to say to Cyrus, too.

"First, I want to thank you for what you have done for Steven," Cyrus began.

"I'm afraid I haven't done much," Elliott objected. "I tried but didn't do a very good job of protecting him. If Gentry hadn't come when he did, we would all be history by now."

"Your coming back started this thing unraveling," Cyrus said. "And it has accomplished much more than you know." He smiled thinly. "And you found out you were part owner of my business. That should mean something."

"I want to discuss that with you," Elliott said, leaning forward earnestly. "Give my share to Gentry. He's a good man and has served you well. And—after all—he really is *your* son."

Cyrus's eyes suddenly narrowed and he said harshly, "And where did you glean this interesting bit of scuttlebutt?"

"Allyssa told us! Tilda told her that you were really Gentry's father but that you wouldn't stoop to marrying a servant, even to give your son a name! You let John marry her instead." In spite of himself, Elliott's ire had risen.

"So, you presume to tell me what I should have done about my own son?" Cyrus said icily.

"So! You admit it then?" Elliott shot back.

For a moment Cyrus locked yes with him and then he laughed softly. "I like what you have become, Elliott. You may find it hard to believe, but I have fought many battles with my conscience at how I treated you when you were a child. But in spite of all of it—and maybe because of it—you have become a son to be proud of!"

Elliott felt his mouth fall open in astonishment. He was struck utterly speechless.

A light glowed in Cyrus's eyes and his voice softened. "How proud Ellen would have been of you. I wish she could see what you have become: strong in body and will, wise, courageous, gentle—yet not a cream puff."

Elliott felt his heart pounding like surf against ocean cliffs. A heady delight swelled up inside his chest, he felt slightly lightheaded. After all these years of longing for any tiny scrap of approval from his stepfather, it had finally come! And he felt like a small child, delirious with joy over Cyrus's words of praise.

As Elliott stared at Cyrus in stupefied wonder, Cyrus suddenly laughed softly. "Don't look so incredulous. I'm just giving you something you should have received from me all your life."

Sudden tears filled Cyrus's eyes, and he dropped them self-consciously, wiping them again with his handkerchief. He spoke as if to himself, "I've done a lot of thinking since Steven was kidnapped. And I realize how foolish I have been! Three fine sons I have been privileged to have under my roof and I only acknowledged Austin.

"And then I proceeded to spoil him until he was of no worth

to anybody—even to himself! How tragic to look back on my folly and know that I failed miserably in the one thing that counted in this life—my family."

Elliott tried to speak but the words seemed to fizzle out in his mouth. His thoughts were all mixed up; his mind reeling. The incredible had happened! How could Cyrus have changed so miraculously in such a short time?

Cyrus slowly took a small book from the large pocket of his robe and held it out to Elliott. "I believe this is yours."

Elliott took the worn, leather-bound book into his hand and stammered, "B–but how did you get this? I thought someone had stolen it!"

"I had Tilda get it for me from your room," Cyrus said slowly. "Ever since you came back, Ellen has seemed to walk the halls of Coppercrest." The words choked off and he swallowed hard several times before he could continue. "For years I told myself I hated her because I thought she loved only your father...never me."

He lifted burning eyes to Elliott. "But after you came back, I finally began to let myself think about Ellen. The things she said and the things she did. And I began to know with certainty that she did love me—in spite of all my black faults."

"Yes, Mother loved you," Elliott said. "I always knew that—and resented it."

"I know you resented me, even hated me," Cyrus said, "and I reveled in that resentment. I think," he said slowly, "that it was easier to hate you—and Ellen—if I felt it was returned. So I deliberately provoked you—and your mother—to anger and to hate. You responded in like manner, but your mother never did."

"Because she had Jesus Christ in her life," Elliott said, then was amazed at his own words. He had never thought about it that way before. Of course that was why Ellen had never hated Cyrus, in spite of his meanness!

"Yes," Cyrus said thoughtfully, "because she had Jesus

Christ in her life. And lately I have begun to want what she had. That's why I had Tilda take your mother's Bible from your room and bring it to me."

His voice trembled. "Did you know Ellen wrote messages to me and you and Austin in her Bible? It was like sitting down and talking to Ellen in person. I could almost hear her voice speaking to me!"

"Yes, I know," Elliott said. "I recently followed the path she laid out in her Bible—with little messages and underlined Scriptures—and found her God!"

Cyrus looked at Elliott silently for a long moment and then down at his long, thin hands. His voice quavered slightly as he said, "I've been wondering if God would really forgive an old fool like me."

A Scripture leaped into Elliott's mind and he quoted it softly, "Whosoever shall call upon the name of the Lord shall be saved."

Cyrus rubbed his face with a weary, shaky hand. "I'm more exhausted than I realized. You must be, too. Why don't you go on up and rest? I–I must give this a little more thought."

"I learned last night that life is very uncertain at best," Elliott said earnestly as he rose to leave. "I wouldn't wait too long."

Late that evening, when the huge, fiery-red ball of the sun was dipping below the hills, turning the sky into a rainbow of breathtaking colors, Lee and Elliott sat in a swing in the little garden. Steven was just beyond the gate, clattering up and down the stone stairway, playing a make-believe game of his own.

Elliott's arm rested lightly about Lee's shoulders, and they were rocking contentedly back and forth.

"I can still hardly imagine the change in Cyrus," Lee said softly. "He wants to go to church Sunday! And he was even kind to me. My father-in-law was always the coldest, most unloving person. If only it will last!"

"I believe he will come to Christ very soon," Elliott said. "And, incredibly, I will be glad! I have hated Cyrus all my life and now God has melted that hate away as if it never existed."

"I guess I hated him, too," Lee said, "but I couldn't hate him now. He–he said I was to be the daughter of the family now," she said with a catch in her voice. "That means more to me than all the money in the world!"

"And he's claiming me for a son after all these years," Elliott said. "I plan to stick around here and lap up some of his affection, too. It's strange that I still want it...even feel a need for it...after all these years."

"Are you going to work at Deadly Gypsy Blue?" Lee asked teasingly.

Elliott turned and looked into Lee's eyes. His eyes were warm. "Yes, I'm a partner and I might as well take advantage of it. Especially since I want to get to know a certain pretty car mechanic/chauffeur lady better!"

Lee's expressive face glowed and her eyes met his steadily. "I would like that," she said softly.

Elliott touched his lips lightly to her forehead and then settled back with a contented sigh. "I've never felt so happy and at peace in my life and I thank God for it all."

"Talking about happiness," Lee said, "did you notice Gentry's face when Cyrus asked Gentry to forgive him for wronging him all these years! And then gave him an equal share ownership in the family business, with you and me and Steven!"

"It literally glowed!" Elliott agreed. "And when he gruffly told Gentry he was proud to claim him as his son, I thought Gentry was going to bawl like a baby," Elliott said. "And I think I did!"

"I know I cried," Lee declared. "And I looked up and saw Tilda wiping her eyes on her apron. Her face was shining like a Christmas tree. She's so proud of Gentry and this is a dream come true for her. Even John seems happy about it—although he was a loving father for Gentry all these years."

"It was a bit of a shock, though, when Tilda admitted to me that she was the one who cut up the cardboard backs of my photographs and threw Mother's Bible down the stone steps," Elliott said.

"I didn't know about that," Lee said. "Whatever for?"

"She said she had always been jealous of my mother because Cyrus had married her instead of Tilda. When I came back, the old feelings were revived. In a fit of anger at Ellen, she threw the Bible down the stone stairs. She was going to cut up the photos, too, she said. But since she did really care about me, she couldn't bring herself to destroy the photos because I treasured them.

"Tilda has always been a sweet person. She made life bearable for me here when I was a child."

"She has a good heart," Lee said.

"I'm hopeful that she and Gentry and John will also come to know Christ." Elliott said. "Gentry's a good man, and I'm pleased he's to retain the managership of Gypsy Blue Enterprises. I want to learn the business from him. I think he trusts me now and knows I don't want to take his job. With all of us working together as a family, I'm excited about the future—and the business. We shouldn't ever have to call her Deadly Gypsy Blue again."

Steven's voice interrupted them. "Uncle Elliott...Mama... come climb the stairs with me."

Smiling indulgently, Elliott and Lee linked hands and went together down the path to the stone stairway.